Denise Enoch Craton

VOLUME #3 OF THE

ENCOUNTERS
OF
SHORT ARISINGS

TRILOGY

BEYOND ENCOUNTERS
BY
DENICE ENOCH CRATON

T.E.J.A.A.D. PUBLISHING BOOKS
www.deniceenochcraton.com

BEYOND ENCOUNTERS
This is a T.E.J.A.A.D. BOOK

The events in this story are either real or fictitious, emerging both from the life of the author and from her vivid imagination. With the permission of some of the persons represented in this story, actual names are used. Other names have been changed.

VOLUME #3 OF THE ENCOUNTERS OF SHORT ARISINGS
TRILOGY
BEYOND ENCOUNTERS
© 2012 Denice Enoch Craton
www.deniceenochcraton.com

Edited by
Adre`nus O'Hara
Dawn Morgan Flores

Cover design © 2012 Adrenus Craton Designs
www.adrenuscraton.com

Published by
T.E.J.A.A.D. Publishing
P. O. Box 757
Hallettsville, TX 77964-4952

All rights reserved.

T.E.J.A.A.D. Publishing, P. O. Box 757, Hallettsville, TX 77964
Toll Free 1-877-798-1838 tejaadpublishing@aol.com

First Edition
Library of Congress Control Number: 2005907355
ISBN 978-0-9755611-7-1

ATTENTION: Quantity discounts are available on bulk purchases of this book. For information, please contact T.E.J.A.A.D. Publishing.

Printed in the U.S.A.

In loving memory of my son, Jadeaus Cory Craton
January 21, 1976 – October 6th, 1999

ACKNOWLEDGEMENTS

Again, I thank the source of the inspiration from which I continue to gain motivation. I am now comfortable in my inner thinking as I had been before the tragedy of my son's death. I will always acknowledge the source which, while in my negative thinking, made me aware of the positive side of the intricate inner workings of my short-term changed mental status, so affected by the loss of Jadeaus. I thought hard upon such inspiration and drew from it as needed while writing Volume III (Beyond Encounters) of the Encounters of Short Arisings trilogy, because this novel covers the details of finding out about Jadeaus' death. What turmoil I was in at the writing of Volume I, The Journey! And now, I find my mind in a more peaceful state, although as I wrote, sad feelings of my dear loss flooded in and outpouring of copious tears was the order of the day. Therefore, it is most appropriate, as in the first instance, to again express this heartfelt appreciation. Everyone should make use of that which inspires, whether it is their own inner inspiration, because it is definitely there, or through the efforts of someone or something that does such inspiring. I shall delve into and make use of *my* source indefinitely. As at the start, I remain inspired and the healing continues.

And now, you, Adre`nus, what an accomplishment! I've enjoyed working with you throughout the trilogy. Once again you have been there at my every beckoning throughout my writing this third novel, with all of your expertise in getting the entire trilogy "out there". I say a heartfelt, thank you so much, for the dedication, hard work and love you extended in helping with my endeavor to complete this trilogy. You expended yourself to no end with the full support of your husband, Eddie. Thank you, Eddie! What a wonderful son-in-law I have in you and what a very supportive husband to my daughter you are! I love you both.

To my son, Tobias and daughter-in-law, Francis, from both of you, I received beautiful prodding along the way. The two of you contributed for a quality work. Your good suggestions came at the right time, every time. I treasure the moments of the carefully spoken words that you, Tobias and you, Francis, chose. They were with graciousness, so to speak, and seasoned with salt, which made them palatable and the end result of taken them to heart is reflected in the outcome of the trilogy. Thank you and I love the both of you.

To my son, Arkus and daughter-in-law, Kari, I appreciate wisdom from the 'young', in that, the input given for the first volume until now this third volume of the trilogy was taken and implemented. Thank you both for being there for me. The two of you are an inspiration to me and an asset to the publishing company, and I look forward to tapping in to more of the great ideas that are sure to come from you two. I love you both.

I would like to thank you, Le`Misha Le`Rae Jenkins, for the times I texted you in the early morning hour, with questions that I needed answers to for my novel; you are much closer to the days of High School than I am. I'm glad you're part of our publishing company and look forward to more of the type of assistance you've already extended with the three volumes. Thank you very much.

Diana Sanchez, I appreciate very much the time you took to proofread this volume before it went to print to assure a quality read for our growing audience of readers. Thank you!

I cannot fail to mention you, Dawn. You put forth much effort, time and energy when you edited Volume III and for that I am so very grateful. What a relaxing atmosphere you provided in your home as we read the manuscript aloud. I appreciated the trips you made from your home in San Antonio to our country home in Hallettsville. I will always treasure the good times we had when we read and edited this novel. Thank you so very much, Dawn. I can hear you now if we were editing this acknowledgment to you. If I had not placed a comma before your name, you would have said, "That's, 'Thank you so very much comma Dawn'." I had to put that in your acknowledgement to preserve just a hint of the fun times we had. You did not have the opportunity to edit this personal acknowledgement I'm expressing to you, so, I hope the training I received while observing you at work on my novels during the past several years will show within this acknowledgement. I have no doubt you will edit it. That's one of the many things I came to know about you; you do enjoy editing. I'm really happy you came onboard our family's publishing company and I truly look forward to working with you in the future. Until then, take good care, my treasured friend.

I must thank Dawn's husband, Mario. Mario, once again you gave up time that could have been spent with Dawn so that she could get my novel ready for publishing. I appreciate the sacrifice you made during our reading and editing, but, especially the bigger sacrifice it took on your part when she took time to edit the novel to get it to where she and I could read it aloud. Thank you very much.

I would like to extend my appreciation to, Leroy and Billie Mae Johnston, for the permission given to use their names as real characters in my novels. I especially thank you, Mrs. Johnston for allowing me to share with my readers a special recipe from your recipe box that belonged to your mother, the late, Christine Repschleger.

I must acknowledge Bill and Emily Jean Applet, the source from which I was able to do the final read of this novel without distraction, at their farm house located on the property of the late, Mr. William Fahrenthold. The deer I saw in the early morning and late evening or the owls hooting late at night were not distractions for me. They were welcomed to the sight and endearing to the ears, memories embedded within. For these cherished memories of my stay in their very nice and cozy farm house, I warmly thank Bill and Emily Jean Appelt. Thank you both for allowing me to have the comfort and the solitude that I needed to complete this trilogy. I will always remember the both of you for it. Thank you!

And to you Elliott, the love of my life, what can I say? The words "thank you", although an expression of the most heartfelt, seem not to say just how much I appreciated your constant support and your positive attitude that I could finish these three volumes. And now, they're done! I release you from the easy chair I conveniently placed in front of my writing desk so as to pull on your listening ear. What a great listener you have been through the years. You have so lovingly, understandingly, and unselfishly supported my writing from day one, and now, see what we, together, have accomplished! It is with the utmost sincerity that I say this: Thank you, Elliott Craton; I love you very much, now and forevermore.

With the closing out of this trilogy I would like to thank you, the reader…

A POEM FOR YOU

There are numerous types of persons as found throughout the entire universe
Those whose desire is to be silent, and then those who would rather converse
One prefers to write, while others choose simply to read, yes life is so diverse
Real thoughts one will inscribe, but the imagined ones are sought to immerse

At one moment or another in time, there is an encounter of someone it is true
Perhaps it was a good impression to remember or one not to be kept as a cue
In any case, encounters of all kinds simply happen, and with them do not rue
Each carries a lesson that is to be learned by any and all who accept this clue

Beyond the encounter lies a telling experience that could only have been told
And also known because one preferred to write and one chose a book to hold
Many people surround each and every one, so to start an encounter is so bold
What goes beyond can be good for the taking it's as valuable as refined gold

Now there has been some type of an enlightening encounter with the writer
Perhaps what you have read will make things for you diminutively lighter
With the first writing I had no preset thoughts that you would hold on tighter
Yet, here you are having made the life of one person in this universe brighter

Thank you, for taking the time to read what I wrote within these past years
Just think if all just wrote, why, a most favorite pastime would not be clear
I do look forward to entertaining you in the years ahead, please have no fear
To finish writing the trilogy was my heartfelt desire. That goal is now here.

NOTE FROM THE AUTHOR

In a span from 1993 to 2005, Volume III of "Encounters of Short Arisings Trilogy," Beyond Encounters, covers what happened to the characters after their very first encounter in Volume I, The Journey. It also covers what is currently taking place to a few of these characters - *This particular novel is more real than it is imagined.* I display more of my vivid imagination as I reveal an unexpected twist, not only to you, the reader, but, also to one of my main characters. More importantly, in a step by step way, I cover my own past real-life experiences that were lodged into the crevices of my own mind, as was the case with Brant Chamberlain and his past. I now share them with my growing audience of readers, from which has come an array of positive, motivational and much appreciated comments. This is what makes reading this third novel a *must*.   Enjoy!

BEYOND ENCOUNTERS

CHAPTER ONE

Brant and Suzanna had spent many late evenings together on their front porch swing and on occasion observed the lights go out at their daughter's house located to the west of their property about half a mile away.

Brant arrived in the United States after answering an online ad for a Texas property promising to 'take your breath away.' His inquiry led to the eager, unhesitant purchase of the real estate that allowed him to relocate. Thereafter, he spent each night sitting on the front porch swing, enjoying the sounds of nightfall in the country, waiting for the lights to go out at his daughter's house. Brant did this before he and Suzanna were reunited, and now the two of them cherished not only their life together, but the fact that they were all together. To have Brant and their two children, Dezeray and Antonio, together as one united family was something that Suzanna had wanted for many years. Brant was so very happy that his long journey in search of Suzanna and Dezeray was now over. It had such a happy ending and was a new beginning for them. Often times Brant looked at Suzanna as she slept. He stared in amazement at how, after all the years that had passed, he still saw his very young bride. He then called to mind how she looked the last time he saw her in Paris, France.

They kissed goodbye that morning before she left for her scheduled flight from Paris' Charles de Gaulle Airport to JFK Airport in New York. Since this was her routine flight, he had no idea that this particular morning would be the last time he would see her – As usual, he dismissed the memory as quickly as it entered his mind and reflected as he looked at her, on how good things had turned out for them.

Autumn became their favorite season to sit on their front porch and swing slowly as they enjoyed together the sights and sounds of country living. Because their house was situated on the highest hill in the area, they enjoyed watching the foliage change across the pasture in the distance. Although what could be seen was not as breathtaking as the vastness and variety of the foliage changes seen in the northeastern part of the United States, their view was nevertheless spectacular. The previous owner of Brant's property had interspersed the land with Maple and Tallow trees, producing a most colorful display. The property could bring satisfaction to any visitor not so fortunate to have such a view. There was something about this particular piece of property, because of how it was groomed, that revealed the attentive diligence of someone well-traveled and very learned about landscaping.

During another favorite time of year, springtime, the property's rolling hills had an abundance of dancing Bluebonnets. It was an inviting scene that beckoned travelers to temporarily interrupt their journey. The beauty of the sea of Bluebonnets brought on a desire for a closer look. Reaching the "Y" in the road leading up to the Chamberlain home, they parked their vehicles on either side of the road and disembarked for a stroll along the fence line to admire the spectacle. Most of the visitors were not from the area and thus were not aware that the road reached a dead-end right at the house. Having snapped several photos or recorded lengthy moving pictures of their walk up the road, turning back afforded them a second view on the way back to their cars and trucks.

On one occasion Brant and Suzanna were amused watching a family that just *had* to climb over the fence to get that perfect vacation photograph of their little girl sitting in amongst the fullness of the Bluebonnets. They also saw another family get a photo of a little brother and sister in the Bluebonnets. They were holding hands as if they were the best of friends, but then, just after the picture was taken, *look out!* It was quite amusing.

Other times, like this morning, Suzanna sat on the front porch swing watching the families and their little ones and was saddened that her memories did not include such happy occasions. She was so young when she gave birth to Dezeray. She and Brant were both in agreement to allow relatives in Texas to raise her. By the time Antonio was born ten years later, remnants of the guilt she felt over giving Dezeray to her Aunt Kathryn resurfaced, so much so that the mental distress grew within her and she began to center her thoughts on being close to Dezeray. Before she was totally consumed with mental distress and not in a position to get the kind of help she knew she needed, she set out to the town in Texas where she knew her Aunt Kathryn lived and where she and her Uncle Donald had taken Dezeray.

She made the trip back and forth to the United States so many times. However, upon her arrival at JFK Airport this-time, she simply quit her job and booked a flight to Victoria, Texas, a small town about forty-five miles south of Hallettsville where she knew Dezeray had been taken. Suzanna longed to be close to her daughter after the fifteen year separation from her. She left Antonio, now five, with Brant's sister, Tese, who frequently assisted in his care. Her plan was to get the help she knew she needed and then inform Brant of her location.

4

Brant could then get Antonio, travel to the States and re-unite the family. She was confident in the outcome.

Immediately upon arrival at the small airport in Victoria, she called her Aunt Kathryn, who was in total shock that Suzanna had successfully made the long trip in her distressed condition. She recognized Suzanna's determination to get help, but after listening to her niece and detecting the desperation in her voice, she surmised that Suzanna's desire for a reunion with her daughter included her need to reveal herself as Dezeray's real mother. It was clear that Suzanna was in need of professional help. Kathryn was relieved that Suzanna had admitted to it.

Suzanna confided her feelings about her mental status and asked where she could go for help. She had absolutely nowhere else to turn. Being aware of this herself, Kathryn decided she would be the one to help her. Through the school program called 'Job Find' Dezeray worked part-time at the Library. It was the afternoon hour and Dezeray would not be in until five o'clock, so Kathryn felt there was ample time to take care of Suzanna.

While on her way to the airport where Suzanna was waiting, Kathryn stopped at the Cranbrook Institution in the city of Yoakum to inquire whether or not there was an opening for a voluntary admittance. She met with one of the doctors on duty and explained Suzanna's situation. He understood, encouraging Kathryn to bring her in, assuring her that they would be more than happy to help.

There would be times while sitting on the front porch on mornings like this that Suzanna would observe scenes with families together taking pictures and her thoughts regressed to her sad past.

So many years had passed, she thought. As the swing slowed almost to a halt, she reminisced about where she and Brant lived from the start of their marriage through the birth of little Dezeray. As she recalled the day that Aunt Kathryn and Uncle Donald arrived at their house in Paris, she could still see their happy faces as Kathryn held Dezeray. On Kathryn's face, however, she remembered seeing mixed emotions. As she looked back, she now recognized that those other expressions and mixed emotions were that of concern for her, as the *so very young mother-child*. The tears Kathryn shed that day were of both happiness and sadness.

Suzanna left the porch swing and went inside. In the nearest mirror she saw in her face the same two expressions that were on Kathryn's face the day she and Uncle Donald picked up Dezeray. Below the mirror was located the family portrait of the four of them. Suzanna stared in the mirror for a long time. Indeed, she did see those same two expressions of happiness and sadness. Even the tears now rolling slowly down her own cheeks resembled those she saw on Kathryn's face so long ago. She was happy to be united with Dezeray once again, yet sad for missing the childhood of her daughter. It was something that she had to come to grips with over the years, and she assured herself that she was determined not to allow any sadness overrule her happiness, not even from observing these scenes of the families that happened onto their property.

Still in the early stages of such determination, Suzanna now found this inner strength that had been dormant. It was a strength that pervaded any situation in which she found herself with anyone or anything that threatened that happiness. It was an inner quality that she had before she left Paris, and then rediscovered during her stay at the Cranbrook institution. She was now ready to command it to action.

Dezeray most assuredly inherited this quality and used it in behalf of her family and loved ones. In turn, her daughter, Adreanna had inherited the same inner strength. Eli and Dezeray watched her manifest it countless times when she dealt with her three brothers, Tory and Arelius, and only on a few occasions, with Jake. Her parents allowed such a manifestation, knowing that she would need these qualities when she pursued her art career in New York.

Three generations of females in this family had that same personality and perhaps four, if including Suzanna's mother, Mama Josephine, as all the grandchildren would call her. Mama Josephine's strong will showed on her face and came out in her actions with everyone.

What also contributed to Adreanna's personality was

the spirited manner of Eli's mother, Alice, as well as Alice's mother, Ruby. It seemed that all the genes making for the energetic, free spirited, feisty and self-confident attitude were set aside especially for Adreanna.

BEYOND ENCOUNTERS

CHAPTER TWO

The time was quickly approaching for Adreanna to join her brother, Tory, in New York. She would not leave Texas without saying goodbye to her brother, Jake, in Eagle Pass. It was a *must do* trip, according to Adreanna.

While growing up, she and Jake were so close, and soon more than two thousand miles would separate them, no doubt for only a short time. With the generous gift given to Jake by his grandfather, Brant, Jake would board a plane to New York to see not only Adreanna, but also Tory and his uncle Lance.

Eli went over all the important details about the feed store with Arelius and felt confident that, with Grandfather Brant and Uncle Arthur looking in on him, he would successfully take care of things.

Eli said to Arelius, "Now Arelius, I'm leaving you in charge of the family business. To do such a thing, first,

I would have to feel you are capable. I feel you are and that you will do a great job. Now the next two things are: Do *you* feel you're capable? Then if so, do you *want* to run the business while your mother and I take Adreanna to say goodbye to Jake?

Arelius always managed to find his chest and stick it out when it came to the praises he got in the company of Adreanna. This occasion was no exception.

"Not to worry, Dad," said Arelius, "I can handle it. I want Little Sis to go say goodbye to Jake before she goes to New York." As he was saying that, his eyes found Adreanna and he smiled like he always did when attention was on him.

It did not matter to Adreanna this time. She wanted to speak the thoughts from her mind: "Yeah, but *you're* going to be working and *I'll* be visiting," but she bit her tongue, not wanting anything to interfere with the good-bye hug she intended to deliver to Jake. After all things were taken care of, the family left for Eagle Pass.

Jake eagerly looked forward to their visit. Although the highlight of the visit was seeing his parents (and his siblings when they would accompany them), Jake looked forward to the frozen meats and other goodies Dez would package up and bring to him. Jake always enjoyed when visitors dropped by with food. The rule was that whatever was left over stayed. He would end up with several bottles of soda, unopened bags of chips, and various sweets, which no doubt accounted for his stocky build. More importantly, Jake was looking forward to seeing Rachel. He called her in Victoria to invite her to come to Eagle Pass to spend time with his family, but most of all to be with him.

The drive to Eagle Pass was dusty and hot, normal Texas weather. It was during those long journeys to see her son that Dez had her moments to reflect on her family, to think about where they'd all be in years to come and also to get some much needed rest while Eli drove.

Jake met his parents and Adreanna at the door and as deep dimples appeared on each cheek, minutes seemed to pass in slow motion as his eyes moved first to Adreanna, then to Dez, then to Eli, finally fixing on the freezer box of his favorite meats from Glen's Meat Market in Hallettsville. The latter caused an even bigger smile and even deeper dimples. He fell into a daze of when he was ten years old and met his best pal, Penny Haggerty, for the first time at the fence line.

Adreanna was compelled to tease at the sight of his eyes glazing over, "What's the matter Jake, is your apartment untidy, unkempt, or do you have female company in there, like maybe, Rachel?" As he came back to reality, standing there in the doorway of his apartment, holding his family at bay, so many thoughts went through Jake's mind. At the mention of Rachel, he was suddenly very present. "Why are y'all still outside? Come on in! And you, little sister, are wrong in all of the above – at least for the moment about whether or not Rachel is in here."

He hugged Adreanna to the sweet delight of Dez and Eli looking on, neither one knowing that this would be their last hug… their last encounter.

"What does that mean?" asked Adreanna, "Will Rachel be coming to Eagle Pass today?"

"Now that you mentioned it, yes, she will be here in a little bit. I told her you were coming to say good-bye to me before you left for New York, and *she* wanted to come to tell you good-bye. Is that alright with Little Sister?"

"I suppose its okay, especially since she's practically here already," said Adreanna.

It was a very good visit for all, and Jake and Adreanna parted, happy to have been together this one last time before she traveled so far away. Rachel did finally arrive and was pleased to be included in the family's special time together.

Although Rachel was a few years younger than Jake, she possessed a level of maturity and common sense that equaled her older companions. Her thick, waist-length hair flowed loosely down her back. She had never applied a stroke of mascara or eyeliner to her very remarkable eyes, but they were always just as beautiful as if she had been made up by one of Hollywood's most renowned makeup artists.

There were many things about her that bore a striking resemblance to Jake. For instance, at the beach on Memorial Day weekend before Tory left for New York, Dez noticed that both Rachel and Jake were left handed. They also had an atypical cowlick located in the exact same spot, on the left side of the head about an inch above the ear, and both had identical dimples on each cheek. *Dimples with an attitude seemed to be a recurring characteristic of all the girls in Jake's life, including his childhood pal, Penny.*

It seemed to his parents, that Jake encountered the most beautiful females in his world. They attributed such encounters, however long, not only to his handsomeness, but also to his caring attitude that was obvious to all. He had a personality that attracted young women like a magnet attracts metal.

Sometime after Jake admitted to his mother that his feelings for Rachel were different than his feelings for his "pal" Penny, Dez had an opportunity to talk with her. During the course of their conversation, Rachel revealed that she was attracted to Jake because of the way he treated his sister. Rachel said that her mother always told her that, when looking for someone to spend the rest of her life with, she should take special note of the man's relationship with his family, especially the one with his sister. Dez agreed with Rachel, and she also shared something with her that she had always told her boys... "How you treat your sister is a good indication of how you'll treat your wife."

Rachel told Dez that Jake let her know he did not have romantic feelings for Penny, long before he found out they were first cousins. When she saw how he treated Penny after the two of them discovered they *were* first cousins, she was impressed - even more so, when she attended his brother's and sister's graduation. She adored the way Jake acted toward his younger sister, Adreanna, on that night. He was so concerned about her welfare when she got her very first car from her grandfather that he told her to follow them to the Internet Café.

Rachel noted that Jake was soft spoken toward Adreanna, and the common sense he displayed in different situations brought smiles inwardly. At times, she had to openly display her amusement at his way with his siblings. She understood what Dez meant when she told her sons that how they treated their sister was a good indicator of how they would treat their wife. Rachel hoped she and Jake would become the best of friends, and that one day their friendship would develop into closer a relationship, maybe leading to marriage and a lifetime enduring far beyond their first encounter.

BEYOND ENCOUNTERS

CHAPTER THREE

When Dez and Eli returned to Hallettsville with Adreanna, they found everything in order, even better than they had left it, especially the feed store which had been left in the capable hands of Arelius. Since their store was located on the opposite edge of town from their home in the country, the three of them dropped by to check in on him.

"I see you didn't burn down our feed store," Adreanna playfully quipped as she strutted by.

"There were only gains here my dear," he replied as he turned to his father, "No losses whatsoever, Dad," said Arelius, "I now know that this is what I want to do – keep the feed store in the family even for your first grandson to run… and his son and so on and so on."

"Excuse me," Adreanna held her nose in the air, and with hands on both hips continued, "Did I miss the birth of your little Jr.? Better still, did I miss your marriage too?" She held one elbow with the opposite hand while resting a tilted chin on a pointed finger, "Oh, let's see...well, well, there *is* no Missus!" Her hands were back on her hips.

"Enough, Adreanna!" scolded Eli, "Arelius is to be commended for his far-reaching goals for the family business. Arelius, you just keep that as your determination. Your mother and I would be very happy for you to continue the family business. We appreciate you for being here while we went to see Jake."

"No problem, Dad, it's what I've been talking to Grandpa Brant about...a lot. He has his own ideas about my future here in Hallettsville," and as he turned his head, looking at Adreanna he continued with a wide smile, "But those ideas have more to do with a future Missus."

"Well, I know my parents love *all* of their grandchildren and will do whatever is needed for each of you," Dez beamed.

Arelius turned suddenly, as if he had just remembered something. "Mom," he said, raising a single finger at Dez, and continuing with a smile, "Before I forget, Uncle Antonio came by with his lady friend, Officer Roby, and her brother who's visiting them. Mr. Roby told me to call him Ian. He said he met Uncle Lance, Valtora and Vantora while on a singing engagement in Paris. They mentioned to him that you wrote poems and he wants to meet you and Dad while he's here. He asked me to put a bug in your ear about writing a song for Uncle Lance and Valtora's wedding."

"Yes, I remember Lance mentioning Mr. Roby while he was in Paris. He called after he had recited a poem that I wrote for him. It was for him to read to Valtora in the event that she said yes to his marriage proposal. While on the telephone he said he and Valtora would let Mr. Roby know that I wrote poems. And now he's here in Hallettsville?! What a small world we live in!"

"Dez," said Eli as he placed his arm around her shoulders, "I have no doubt that you'll write more than poems. You have a story to tell, and I just know that someday you'll write a book about it."

"I'm thinking seriously about doing just that honey, and you'll be the main character in it," Dez said lovingly to Eli as she put her right palm on his left cheek. The two of them seemed to be in a world of their own.

"Oh well, I guess you guys should get back to the house before customers come in and see our love struck parents making advances toward each other in broad daylight." Arelius laughed.

"And in a public place, I might add." Adreanna giggled, and then crossed her arms in faux disgust. "I can't believe I just agreed with you, Arelius, I must be losing it."

"No, you're just now coming around to seeing things my way after all these years."

"Oh, I can identify with that all right. Like how

you came around to my way of thinking about eight years ago when you gave me my twiddling pillow case…after you bit off all my nails?" asked Adreanna under her breath out of the hearing of Eli and Dez.

Arelius made a facial expression just like the ones he made back when they were younger. Adreanna knew that she had the upper hand of their conversation, which ended abruptly.

Eli and Dez always knew when they were not supposed to know what was going on between the two of them.

The ringing of the telephone interrupted the reminiscing, and with the receiver to his ear, Arelius used a sarcastic tone of voice. "It's Uncle Antonio *again*, for you, Mom."

Antonio was not amused. "I heard that… don't get a big head because someone is interested in *you* – more than the three generations of Tippies in your woodpile."

"I guess *you're* happier now that *you* have a girl on your arm, than when you had that scope around your neck with *no* girl on your arm."

Dez took the phone, breaking the sparring over the phone lines. "Excuse me. I'll take that call now. Thank you, dear. Hello there, Antonio. Is everything alright?"

"Yes, things are fine. I guess we'll be asking that question for a long time. I just wanted to tell you that Michelle's brother, Mr. Roby, wanted to meet with you and talk about writing a song for Lance and Valtora's wedding. I met him yesterday in his mother's hospital room when I went by to visit her. You know Dez, I have no doubt that you may have already written a poem for them and if that's the case, your work is done and it's all up to Mr. Roby to do the singing."

"You're probably right."

"Well, I have to go now. Michelle and I are going out to dinner and her brother is coming along."

"That's nice, Antonio – a chaperone. No wonder her mother likes you."

"Perhaps she does. Oh by the way, how was Jake?"

"He was well." Dez was pleased with his interest. "Rachel, the beautiful young girl you met at the house on graduation night made a trip there to say goodbye to Adreanna. No doubt Jake was happy to see her."

"That's good, Dez. Well, I'd better go now. We'll talk soon. I have more to talk to you about when we can get together. I'll let Mr. Roby know that you'll give him a call. Oh, that reminds me, he gave me the number where he's staying while he's here in Hallettsville."

"Thank you," Dez said, "if you give it to me now, we'll give him a call when we get to the house."

BEYOND ENCOUNTERS

CHAPTER FOUR

Following his wonderful time in Paris, Ian Roby made his way back to the United States to visit his ailing mother, now being attended to by his sister, Michelle, while in treatment in a small hospital in Texas. During the flight from Paris to New York, he had an intriguing encounter with a man named Evan Kinkaid who also had an interest in Texas. They parted ways in New York and Ian caught his connecting flight to San Antonio, where he intended to spend a short time visiting an old friend before traveling further to be with his family.

He arrived at the airport and sought out the car rental window. As soon as he drove the car out of the lot, he observed a San Antonio Police Department vehicle in his rear view mirror. He muttered his favorite lines, *What? What did I do?* The police car was behind him for the better part of his ride, as if escorting him to his desired destination. Then, seemingly in a moment less than an escaping breath, the lights began to flash as the police car zoomed past him. He realized that the policeman was simply in pursuit of the vehicle that had just sped past them both.

With a sigh of relief, Mr. Roby continued on in hopes of soon having an ice cold Pepsi. Just in case his friend had none, and dreading the thought of not having his thirst quenched, he looked for his next opportunity to exit the freeway to find a convenience store. He stopped at the next available service station. He began to think about his previous conversation with the friend he had called from Paris, letting him know he was traveling to Texas to see his mother.

*Yes, today is Wednesday, the day I told him I'd be here. But, you know I can't believe this; I told him I'd be here **next** week Wednesday. How did that happen? I have a very good guess how it happened. My mind has been a little off lately. Vantora-on-the-brain has been the reason for my past three miscalculated appointments. First, I missed that appointment with Mr. Haggerty the other day while in Paris about the very thing I do...sing. Thank goodness he was kind enough to reschedule our meeting. Then there was my barber appointment. What was I thinking walking in there five hours after the scheduled appointment? And to top it all off, I was sure I arrived early for my flight, but was actually six hours late. I'd say what attributes to this confusion going on* *with you, Ian Roby, sounds like Vantora. I guess I should just keep right on driving to Hallettsville after I stop here and get my cold Pepsi. That'll be too long of a drive without it. I'm not even going to call him. That would be a bit embarrassing for me, and who knows what that outgoing guy is doing today anyway? Next week will be just fine; besides, I can't wait to see Mom and Michelle.*

"Not another one," said Mr. Roby quietly to himself as he was exiting his car. *San Antonio is crawling with cops*, he thought as he greeted the officer coming out of the store.

"Hello sir."

"Hey! Nice car!" said the officer, nodding his head.

"Thanks," said Mr. Roby, "I've seen quite a few of you patrolmen out today."

The policeman stood close to Mr. Roby's car.

"Yeah, this is nothing like the small town I was transferred from. All there was to worry about out there was a complaint that someone had walked across their grass, or someone held a parking space for more than two hours. Oh, occasionally there was a bigger issue to deal with, but by far, the majority of the time things were a lot slower than here."

"Well, I'm headed to a small town about a hundred miles from here. My mother broke her hip and was taken there to be near my sister, who is also in law enforcement."

"A hundred miles from here?"

"Yes, well, about that many." Ian nodded and shifted his stance.

"A sister in law enforcement transferred there?"

"Yes, but I can't remember the name of the little town. I always associated it with a friend's name, Hal. My mother is recuperating nearby in a place called Yoakum?" He was unsure.

"Ah yes...well, well, well, you're heading to my old stomping grounds, Hallettsville."

"Yes, that's it, Hallettsville!" Mr. Roby exclaimed, snapping his fingers.

"Okay, I'm curious now. Seems you know more about me than I know about you. Want to level it out?"

"Your sister, would she happen to be Michelle Roby?" The officer paused while waiting for the affirmative answer he was sure would come.

"Yes," said Mr. Roby thoughtfully, turning his ear toward the officer, waiting for him to continue.

"What a small world we live in," the officer said as he shook his head.

"Now where have I heard that recently?" asked Mr. Roby as he thought of Vantora.

"I agree. I take it you're familiar with Hallettsville?"

"Yes, yes I am. How *interesting* meeting you here, in all of San Antonio," said the officer. "My name is Bob Lacy, the former Chief of Police of Hallettsville".

He smiled broadly and extended his hand.

"I'm Ian Roby. Nice to meet you, sir."

"It's nice to meet you too, Mr. Roby."

"Please, Ian will do."

"Alright Ian, Bob will do."

"You've got it, Bob. What are the chances of this happening? This is too much. I was already eager to get to Hallettsville, now I'm more eager to let Michelle know we've met."

"Please, give her my regards. Oh, and will you tell her that I'm still all ears about that unsolved case I had to leave behind? She's supposed to let me know when she cracks it." He slid behind the steering wheel of the cruiser and closed the door.

"I noticed you said *when* she cracks it. It'll only be a matter of time with my li'l sister. She thrives on un-solved cases."

"So she tells me." Bob touched the brim of his hat as he nodded toward Ian and put the cruiser in gear.

"Well, I hope you find your mother progressing to a full recovery. Have a safe trip."

"Thank you officer- I mean Bob. Have a great day!"

"You're welcome Ian; you have a great one too."

Within two hours Ian Roby was in Hallettsville. He was surprised that there on the outskirts of this small town loomed a sprawling University. Every newcomer to Hallettsville felt the same surprise.

He had no problem finding the police department. The thought dawned on him that if his friend was expecting him to visit him *next* week; Michelle would be surprised to see him as well. And surprised she was when he entered the department and they met face to face. Elated, they held each other in an extended warm embrace in the sight of and to the delight of the entire office staff.

"Come to my office!" Michelle exclaimed gleefully as she finally released her embrace.

"But Officer," Ian pleaded, mocking a sad, concerned voice, hands in the air, "It wasn't me. I didn't do it."

Onlookers laughed as Michelle grabbed her brother's left hand and literally dragged him through the door, into her office. Because they were so excited to see each other, both raised a hand to stop the other, so that each could have their say.

His sister poured a cup of coffee. Ian sat in an old armchair hidden in a dimly lit corner of the room. He told her of his meeting with Bob Lacy earlier that day and conveyed his regards. He reminded her that the officer expected to hear *when* she solved that particular case.

Frowning, she sat her cup down.

"Speaking about that case," she said handing her brother his coffee, "I think I have it all figured out, Ian. But the thing is, I don't understand why it happened, especially because of a certain person that I'm sure was involved with it. May I talk off the record with you about it?"

"Sure, 'Chelle. Do I detect a conflict of interest looming?"

She was pacing. "I tell you the truth, Ian; you can read me like a book. You always have been able to do that."

"Well? Go ahead." He sat up in his chair, his interest peaked. "Talk to me."

She continued to pace back and forth in front of her desk. "When I first got here I went directly to the unsolved files. As I read through them, I came across the one Bob Lacy briefly told me about. It intrigued me…so many loose ends. Yet the answers must all be right in the file itself. Perhaps if he had had more time to work on it before he left, Bob would have solved it himself."

Absently, Ian drummed his fingers on his knee.

His sister continued, "I feel I have it worked out, and most of the time when I have that feeling about a certain case it turns out to be right on, but there are still questions that need to be answered. First and foremost, by the one against whom the crime was committed. That person is no longer in Hallettsville."

Ian sat back placing his elbow on the arm of the chair and rested his chin on his fist. "Would you need to have the answers to proceed with the case?"

"I would *like* to have them, just to better understand the involvement of a certain person."

"I see. Although this *is* off the record, perhaps we can talk more about this away from these walls."

Sighing deeply, Michelle replied, almost in a whisper, "I agree." She motioned for him to stand and follow her. "Would you like to go to the house first, or to the hospital?

"Let's go to the hospital first."

"Okay, and by the way, we're going out to dinner tonight with Antonio."

"What am I - a third wheel?" He feigned offense. "If Vantora were here, we'd both accompany you, but she's still in Paris with Valtora. Dinner with the two of you sounds better than eating alone. "

Michelle grabbed his elbow as they emerged into the parking lot. "I've been hearing bits and pieces about you and Vantora. Is it serious?"

"Yes, it is."

"Well, that's about the first time you've given me a straight answer when I've asked you about your life. I see that it *is* serious. Will she be back before you leave?"

Michelle raised her right eyebrow.

"No, we'll *just* miss each other. I have a singing engagement next weekend. It's a "must show" appearance that's been on the books for some time now. But we'll get together soon thereafter. She has invited me to join her, along with Tory and his friends in Spain. I've taken her up on that invite and I'm looking forward to seeing her again. She's the one special person I have in my life now, 'Chelle. She was raised right, just like you and me. She's a good person and we would do good comedy together from some of the things we've experienced since we met. I'll have to tell you about it after dinner tonight."

"Okay," she replied as they turned onto the main road. "Now let's get going."

There was not a police car in sight as they drove the short tour through Hallettsville, at least not until they turned the corner and entered the one-way street around the beautiful historical courthouse. There, parked in front of the Internet Café, Ian saw several police cars. He smiled.

"Is Mom getting better?" Ian asked, breaking the silence.

"Oh yes, and when she sees you, she'll be ready to walk the halls even more. No really, she's doing well."

"And what about Michelle, how's *she* doing?" asked Ian.

"She's doing better than she's done her whole life. She's just where she wants to be at this stage of her life, and found the one she has been searching for."

"You- I mean, *she* could not have been looking *that* long! How old is *she* anyway?"

"You know, she never told me," said Michelle as she smiled her way out of answering directly.

"She's very happy. No, seriously Ian, I am truly happy. Be happy for me. You'll like Antonio. We'll get through this."

"Get through that case you're working on?" Ian asked gently.

"Right again. I'm patient. I don't have all the facts, but I feel they are forthcoming," replied Michelle.

Ian put his arm around her shoulders. "I think a lot of what you say. So let's just leave it at that. I won't push any further," said Ian.

"That sounds good to me. Say Ian, Antonio let his sister know…."

"Dez right?" interrupted Ian, very pleased that he was in the know.

"Yes, you're up on everything aren't you?"

"I do try, li'l sister."

"He told her you were coming to town *next* week," said Michelle.

"Yeah, I meant to apologize right off about arriving a week early. I've been confused lately."

"Ian Roby! You're not *that* old! It must be Vantora."

"I've come to that conclusion too," he confessed.

When the two of them arrived at the hospital, they found their mother with a visitor. It was a visitor whom Ina Roby had begun to think of as a prospective son-in-law. Right off, Ian was impressed that this young

29

doctor had taken to his mother and had been bringing her fresh flowers since their first encounter. After seeing how this man interacted with their mother, Ian had no further reason to wonder what kind of person Antonio was. It was an open and shut case of acceptance that he may be a future member of the family. Antonio also witnessed the loving, caring way Ian interacted with his mother, and that spoke volumes to Antonio as well.

With all of these revelations, Ian, Michelle and Antonio went by the feed store while Eli, Dez and Adreanna had been visiting Jake in Eagle Pass.

Arelius liked Mr. Roby from the very beginning, and the feeling was mutual. Arelius assured Mr. Roby that he would give his mother his message.

When they arrived home, Dez called Mr. Roby to speak with him about writing a song for him to sing at Lance and Valtora's wedding. Dez invited him out to their house the next day to talk about it.

The night before Mr. Roby arrived; Dez went through her poems and found one that she had modified into a song that would make a nice ballad for two people, ready to embark on a life together. It was entitled "Your Eyes to Mine". While sitting at her writing desk she began to read over it:

Your Eyes to Mine

Your eyes to mine have found my imagination
I have longed to look deep into your eyes
What do I discover as you look back at me?
The most intense happiness I have ever ever known,
Stares in my direction yes baby girl our love is full blown
Allow its determination yes, allow its sense
Baby you have no reason with me to be apprehensive,

Don't hold back no don't you furl
As you place your eyes to mine, oh baby girl,
Your eyes to mine (is what I want, so) please,
Look in my direction the way you know how
Let's make our love last and soon we'll be together
Yes baby girl I want your eyes to mine.... cause

CHORUS: Your eyes to mine have found my imagination
As I look into your eyes what do I see
What do I find; you are so radiant to me
Yes baby girl I want your eyes to mine

Entreat me more and more not to lose our intent
This gaze as we lock this most precious moment.
Never let go of your eyes to mine oh no no no
I love you so...believe me when I say,

My eyes are on you, to you, for you, with you,
Let's never part ways oh no my girl, ... cause

CHORUS: *Your eyes to mine have found my imagination*
As I look into your eyes what do I see
What do I find you are so radiant to me
Yes baby girl I want your eyes to mine

Let's just gaze and see what the future hold
I promise to keep you warm yes you'll never be cold
I want to share these feelings about you with the world
Forget about how things will be like tomorrow
Forget about the past let there be no sorrow
As we look into each other's eyes and feel a (great joy)...cause

CHORUS: *Your eyes to mine have found my imagination*
As I look into your eyes what do I see
What do I find you are so radiant to me
Yes baby girl I want your eyes to mine

When she finished making her final changes, she retired to Eli who was awaiting not only her arrival but, also the goodnight kiss he was accustomed to receiving. As soon as she kissed his cheek he dropped off to sleep. Dez watched him appreciatively for a while and after assuring herself that his dreams would be peaceful, she fell into a sweet sleep herself.

The next day, as agreed, Mr. Roby followed the directions given to him and arrived as punctually as he would have for a singing engagement. Eli and Dez were happy to finally meet Mr. Roby, after which, Dez spent the remainder of the afternoon with him writing the song that he would sing at the spring wedding. Before Mr. Roby left, he spoke to Eli and Dez about his feelings for Vantora.

They listened to Mr. Roby go on and on about Vantora, how they met, the time they spent with each other in Paris, and how much the both of them liked each other. Dez decided that the original poem she had modified into a song for Valtora and Lance, "Your Eyes to Mine", would be better suited for *Vantora* and *Ian*. She took a few minutes to edit the modified poem and gave it to him. He read it and thanked her for such a kind deed. Then, based on what they collectively knew about Lance and Valtora, they worked on a song for them.

Later that evening, Antonio, Michelle, and Ian went out to dinner. Antonio had gathered a small amount of information about Michelle the day he initially "interviewed" her mother at the hospital. Additionally, while at the Internet Café, Michelle overheard a conversation between Brant and his brother, Arthur, about Antonio. This small bit of information only made them eager to get to know each other.

Something Antonio first noticed was the fact that her brother, Ian, and their mother, Ina, had the same three letters in their name. He mentioned it to Mrs. Roby, but not in an effort to gain more brownie points because she was already won over the moment he stepped into her hospital room. Even if all the gifts he brought were *not* for her, there was something about Antonio that she took a liking to. She could not quite figure out why, but she hoped her daughter and that young man she had just barely met would continue on together even after *their* first encounter.

BEYOND ENCOUNTERS

CHAPTER FIVE

When Vantora returned from Paris after her one-month stay with her twin sister Valtora, she returned with far more things going on in her life than when she had gone to Paris.

When she arrived back in Hallettsville, she discovered several pieces of mail notifying her to pick up certified letters from the Post Office. In fact, one piece of mail showed three attempts to deliver notices from the Internet Café. After getting settled in at home, she went straight to the Post Office with the notices in hand. After securing the letters, she opened the one from the Internet Café and began to read it in an undertone:

"Dear Miss Vantora Kessley:

Over the past few years it has been a great pleasure having you as our employee. However…

When she read the word, *"However..."* Vantora thought, *I think I don't have a job anymore.* She thought, *I hope the reason for dismissal isn't a negative one. It wouldn't look good on any future résumés I may submit for employment. I was going to quit, but I would like to have done it before they let me go.*

After those fleeting thoughts she continued to read the letter:

"However, at this time it has become necessary for my wife and me to sell the Internet Café. You came to mind as a prospective buyer of our establishment."

Immediately Vantora began to smile with wide-eyed excitement. She did not finish reading the letter. Her only thought was, well, she had many thoughts. One of them was to go home and tell her parents the news. So many thoughts were coming and going. In between each thought was Ian Roby. *But do I want to teach or own the Internet Café? Ian Roby. What about Madrid? What about Ian Roby? Val's wedding and all the preparation for it. Ian Roby.* She did this all the way to her house. She was excited and it showed. She had decisions to make.

On the way back to the States, while the plane was crossing the Atlantic, Vantora looked around and knew he was not to be seen. She had hoped that she would see Mr. Roby. She reflected again on when she and Ian first met. It was a memory she would never forget. She had so much more to decide upon, completely unaware of the letters that awaited her in Hallettsville.

Vantora would check her e-mail daily. On one occasion, she came across a few e-mails in answer to her having applied for Foreign Language positions at several Universities. She had in mind a more mature audience, although teaching at Hallettsville High School was already a challenge for her. But now, she wanted an even more challenging venture, and teaching at a University of her choice was in order.

One of the e-mails was from the University of a favorite country she had visited numerous times, the University of Madrid, Spain. Teaching there would enable her to be in a country that had won a favorite place in her heart over the years.

When she thought of Madrid, she also thought of Tory, whom she had invited to come for a visit after she left Paris. She also thought of Ian Roby because she had invited him as well.

Madrid, Spain, came to be of interest to Vantora while she was a student in Hallettsville High. In her Spanish II class she had the opportunity to go for a two-week vacation catered by the local Advancement in

Spanish Culture Co Ed organization, headed by the distinguished Mr. Sergious Martique, President of the local Chamber of Commerce. He contributed the all-expense paid Junior-Senior trip to Madrid, Spain. Vantora, at the time, was a bubbling junior who learned the Spanish language quickly.

The two groups of students were to stay at the prestigious Hacienda of Mr. Martique. Sergious had come to the States in 1972 and settled down in Hallettsville, Texas, although he kept his Hacienda in the family. He intended to pass it down to his young daughter who was the same age as Vantora. Her name was Miracles. It was a name given to her because her parents considered her to be their small miracle. She came to be called Mila. Mila and Vantora became the best of friends.

Mr. Martique had always wanted to do something for the advancement of knowledge of the Spanish language. With Vantora's keen interests in Spanish, it could not have worked out more perfectly for her. His Advancement Program was to be implemented in her junior year.

In the first year of the program when the two groups of students arrived in Madrid and were taken on a tour of the city, each landmark made an impression on her heart that would not be forgotten. She simply fell in love with Madrid.

It was a place Vantora daydreamed about in her

other classes, only to be brought back to the present situation when her teachers would say, "Vantora Kessley, you've been back from Madrid for how long now? Please pay attention." That expression was mostly heard in her World History class.

When looking at Montana, she saw Madrid, when looking at Massachusetts she saw Madrid, when she saw Mexico, she saw Madrid. She even saw Madrid when the material assigned covered San Antonio.

In her senior year Government class, she memorized everything for her tests, because it was common knowledge that her teacher, Mr. Bissonet, used each exercise at the end of each chapter to give his students their tests. Consequently, she always finished her tests early. This allowed time before the bell to muse over her last year's trip to Spain and to contemplate the next one.

When Vantora got to her house, just before she got in the door, she was calling for her mother. As usual, Mrs. Kessley appeared with apron on. Vantora had to laugh at her appearance as her mother came into the living room from the kitchen. There was what appeared to be flour on her right earlobe. At the sight of it she said to her mother, "I know for a certainty that you have no idea why I'm laughing."

Her mother said, "Vantora, I tell you the truth, you are getting smarter every time I see you. So now, why are you laughing?"

"You have flour on your right earlobe."

"Why do I feel there's more to this than you're saying?"

"Because there is."

"Well, let's sit and talk about it. It'll give me a break from the kitchen."

"Okay. So glad to help you out."

Vantora related all that had happened on the plane with Mr. Roby and during her stay in Paris, at which point the table turned on Vantora. Mrs. Kessley began laughing at Vantora. Vantora's expression turned to a frown. Her mother was hysterical over the fact that her daughter fell into the men's restroom at the Sofitel Paris Arc de Triomphe Hotel while pressing her ear to the door trying to listen to Mr. Roby sing *Lately*.

It was a lot to cover with her mother about Ian Roby. Her mother told her that after dinner the two of them would do the *girlie talk*. It was something they did from time to time, before bed, all throughout the twin's childhood. Mrs. Kessley would jump on their bed, like she was one for a sleepover, and fall asleep with them as if the conversation was strenuous enough to produce tiredness and sleep. Anyone listening would know from the laughter coming from the twin's room that sleep would follow such loud outbursts sooner or later. Mr. Kessley would always bang on the door to awaken Mrs. Kessley and beckon her to bed. The girls had a lot of fun with their mother over the years, and tonight after

40

dinner would be another time when Vantora and Mrs. Kessely would have such a conversation.

"Okay, need help with dinner?" Vantora asked.

"No, thanks. Thank goodness for ovens."

They both laughed as they parted, Mrs. Kessley to the kitchen and Vantora to her bedroom. Vantora remembered that she hadn't told her mother about the prospect of acquiring the Internet Café. She wondered just what it was that had distracted her for the duration of their conversation, and then she realized that it was Ian Roby. *Yes,* she thought, *Ian Roby is on the brain once again. I think I'll start a letter to him right now.*

"Mr. Ian Roby
Entertainer, Side job: Clown,
Day job: Professional Singer"

"Ian," she wrote, "It hasn't been that long ago since we spoke. I truly did hope we would keep in touch. I feel the reason our first encounter has lasted this long is because the first impression we made on each other was just as the expression goes, 'first impression is, the lasting impression.' It has lasted, and it is as vivid as a yesterday's occurrence. I will never forget that impressive first encounter as we flew over

41

the Atlantic and met aboard Air France Flight #1060. What are the chances that we would meet there, or then? I think of how small the possibility and, oh my, it scares me to the point of total frightfulness. During the time I've gotten to know you, you've taken a special place deep within my heart. I look and see you are still there, and it makes me smile. I know you're not trapped there because you do have the key to my heart and I will never change the lock, ever."

"I remember the night you asked me to join you up front at the Hotel's restaurant. One of the lines in the song remains in my mind, as if it were my own name - '*No one really knows whether time will make us strangers or whether time will make us grow.*' It's the part of the song when you came down off stage and sang that line right to me. We discussed it then, and now time has passed and the latter part of that passage is true. You have grown on me so."

"You told me that night out on the patio to speak from my heart. You said it does a body good. You were right. It has contributed to the growth between us, this very good feeling I have about you. You also said you wanted us to keep in touch, and that you would never be 'the saw that cut down the tree that represents our friendship and perhaps in time our relationship.'"

"I think of how things have been going with us and I smile when I think of your sense of humor. I cannot think of anyone with as quick a wit as you. It's a quality I hope you always keep and one that makes for the lively relationship we're cultivating."

"I appreciated your illustration about the saw and the tree. My dad planted a tree before I left. Now, as I am back, when I look at it, I think of what you said. It's tender like our relationship, and will need tender loving care, with plenty of watering and sunshine. I don't know how much truth is in it, but some people attribute the nice healthy growth of some plants to their responding to the sweetness of a calm voice."

"You say you love my smile? I love your voice. With your voice as the watering, and my smile as the sunshine, that should make for a healthy relationship for us."

"Just recently when we were exchanging e-mails into the wee hours of the morning, I told you not to change. You came back immediately and said you couldn't change and that you were the way you were because of your mother and how she raised you."

"I can't wait to hear you again. Valtora also invited me to New York when you go there for your singing performance at Lance's restaurant. I didn't tell her that you had already invited me. I let her think that she's match-making. She thinks there's something to having been born first."

"I'm looking forward to my trip to New York. I hear you now saying 'New York? What about me?' So, yes, I mean I'm looking forward to hearing you, I mean *seeing* you."

"I guess it's time to shut my writing down. Take care of yourself, Ian Roby."

"Vantora (just one word) - smile"

BEYOND ENCOUNTERS

CHAPTER SIX

After sealing the letter to Ian, she enjoyed a dinner with her parents and a long mother-daughter talk afterwards. She then retired to bed returning her thoughts to the Internet Café. Adjusting the pillows, she reached for the letter that she had placed on her nightstand, slipped between the cool sheets and began to read.

"…My wife and I want to offer the Internet Café to someone who we feel will appreciate the historical landmark that it is, being built and restored from the late 1800's, and who will have a good rapport with the townspeople of Hallettsville. They have come to expect home town friendliness from our place."

"If it were not for the fact that our leaving Hallettsville is imperative, you would not have this letter in your hands right now. However, it has become necessary for us to pack up and move."

"If you are interested, we would appreciate meeting with you to further enlighten you about the how's and why's of our imminent departure."

"We look forward to hearing from you, even if you choose not to take us up on our offer."

"Thank you.
Sincerely,
Chase and Gwen Kaiser."

Vantora knew this was a major decision that awaited her attention, but at this moment she just could not focus on all the issues she had to consider. She decided instead to look at the rest of the mail she picked up from the Post Office, those that were from various Universities, wondering what the responses to her teaching applications might be.

She opened the one envelope with a New York State return address and noticed that it had come from New York University. She was pleased to discover a very attractive offer featuring a complete package catering to her every need, and even a few extras.

In her Spanish classes Vantora was an Honor Student throughout High School. Throughout college, at the University of Hallettsville, she mastered Spanish and spoke the language fluently.

Madrid University, like New York, sent a positive reply offering her a position as a Spanish professor. She had totally forgotten she had sent the online application because she was skeptical that such a prestigious University would even consider her.

Of the two, Madrid was more appealing. She felt honored that she had a positive response from there, a place she had loved for many years. When she thought about Madrid, she remembered that another encounter with Ian Roby was in the offing.

Spain would certainly be a wonderful place. As she continued pondering over the rest of the unopened envelopes, she came to the realization that perhaps she just might prefer to be there as a visitor, relaxed and under no pressure, rather than being obligated to the routine of a teaching commitment.

However, while considering New York, she smiled as she thought of Tory, now living there, and how they had become close friends on their first encounter at the Internet Café in Hallettsville. With Valtora's upcoming wedding and her subsequent permanent move there, New York exerted a challenging pull.

Now, lying in bed back in her own house, Vantora

eagerly looked forward to the next time she and Ian Roby would cross paths. This train of thought took her from there, still comfy in her bed and getting a bit sleepy, to her encounter at the Charles De Gaulle airport when she was returning home from her Paris vacation. She had gone to the Starbuck's counter for an iced coffee and while there, she dropped a copy of Dez's novel, "The Journey". A man wearing a derby hat, very gentlemanly, picked it up, and after a quick glance asked, "New author?"

Vantora was caught off guard a bit because first, he picked it up at all, and second, that he spoke to her.

"Yes, a new writer out of Texas," she managed to blurt out.

The mention of Texas interested him more than the book.

"I met a man on my way to Texas not too long ago," he continued as he handed her the book. "He was headed there to see his mother who had broken her hip and was recuperating near her daughter. Interesting how that is."

"What's that?" asked Vantora. She paid the cashier and moved aside for the man to step up and order, but continued to stand near enough to hear his answer.

"Up until my father died recently, I had no interest in the States, not to mention that little town in Texas called Hallettsville that I visited. Had it not been for the fact that my father had business there, talking with you today wouldn't have brought about a connection with Texas."

Vantora was surprised to hear he had been in Hallettsville, of all places. "Did I hear you correctly? Did you say Hallettsville?"

"Yes, I did! And now here's the part where you tell me that's where you're headed," said the man as he sipped at his coffee.

"That's where I'm headed! That's where I live! You said you met a man not too long ago, going there?"

"Yes, I met him while on the plane from Paris. I'm afraid I disturbed him a few times getting up. His name escapes me right now, but he said he was a singer. Poor guy was reading a letter - from his sweetheart I gathered."

At that point, Vantora smiled and slightly lowered her head.

"And I take it from the way you're shying away, that letter was from you."

"I would venture to say yes, it was from me. His name is Ian Roby. And now I'll say it's a small world. My name is Vantora," she said as she extended her hand to the man.

With a firm handshake he responded, "Well, I'm Evan, and it's a pleasure to meet you, Vantora."

The announcement that Vantora's flight for Houston was ready for boarding interrupted their conversation. She gathered her things, shook Evan's hand and said, "I'll have to let Mr. Roby know about this."

Evan offered her a slight bow. "Have a safe flight. Perhaps we will meet again."

She yawned and shifted positions in her bed, fluffing her pillows again and adjusting the blankets. She used the rest of the night to reminisce about more Paris memories, especially the memories with that certain singer who filled the room with his all-consuming voice...She longed for another encounter with him.

Suddenly she was no longer sleepy. First, she sat up, and then she got out of bed and sat at her computer. Opening up the internet, she searched for landmarks in Spain in the area where she would be staying. When she made regular trips to Madrid, she stayed at Mr. Martique's hacienda, with his daughter, Mila. Even if Mila or her family were away, it was understood that Vantora was welcome to stay in their home. They often told her, "Mi casa, es tu casa," which means, "My home is your home". They were enthused that Vantora had not only taken up the Spanish language, but she spoke it exclusively while visiting.

While she was browsing for the different landmarks, she felt happy that her young friend, Tory, was also bilingual. She figured that anything he might miss while becoming adept with the language, his friend, Fran, would translate for him. She chuckled as she recalled how well he understood her sarcastic greeting at the Internet Café the night of his brother's and sister's graduation, something the two of them will not forget.

All she wanted to do this night was locate several places online so that she would have a good reason to discuss them with Ian. And while on the telephone with him, she would let him know about a letter she would send to him in the morning. She located quite a few attractions within a short time and hurriedly went to the telephone.

"Hello, Ian?"

"Yes. Van?"

"Yep, it's me," she said with a large grin that could be heard in her voice.

"I'll never forget that southern voice."

"How are you, Ian?"

"I'm good, Van, and you?"

"So am I. I'm actually making an itinerary for my trip to Madrid and thought about my invitation to you. Will it be a go on your end?"

"Yes, and I must say I'm looking forward to visiting with you in Spain."

"Great! There are a few points of interest you may like to see while there." She began a visual scan of the list on her screen.

"Oh? Perhaps you can e-mail a list of them to me. I'd like to get some more information."

"You know, that's exactly why I was calling you. If some interest you more than others, just prioritize them and we'll see how far we get on our tour: From the Museo Nacional Centro de Arte Reina Sofia, translated, *Queen Sofia Arts Center* to the many architectural buildings and amusement parks...especially the Aquasur water park for Tory and his friends...well, it may take a few visits for you to see *all* of Madrid."

"That's not a bad idea. I've heard a lot about Jardin Botanico. I'd love to see that garden and use the Teleferico to get there."

"My, Ian, I do believe you are already familiar with the place."

"Yes, a bit. I'd also like to check out the Kapital, that seven story attraction. Want to put that on your itinerary for dining?"

"Okay, I will."

"Oh, and one more place I'd like to see while there."

"Yes?"

"The Palacio Real, translated, *Royal Palace*. I hear it's a luxurious, over-the-top, decorative palace with over two thousand lavishly gilded rooms. A historic site for sure," Ian said while trying very hard not to give himself away.

"Ian?"

"Yes, Van?"

"I think you've already done your research, and quite well I must add."

"Hmmm, I do think you caught me there, darlin," said Ian, in a southern tone. Clearing his throat of nothing, he said, "Changing the subject since I've been found out, I miss you, Van. I'm looking forward to seeing you again."

"I miss you too, Ian, and it was refreshing to hear your voice. Let's talk again soon."

"That would be nice. You take care."

"Thanks, you too. Bye, Ian."

"Bye, Van."

BEYOND ENCOUNTERS

CHAPTER SEVEN

Lance left Paris in hopeful anticipation of his next encounter with Valtora. After she accepted his marriage proposal, together they chose Spring as the season for their wedding. Her twin sister, Vantora, was chosen as her maid of honor and would be escorted down the aisle by Ian. Lance's time away from his dearest love was filled with vivid images of their wedding day and of how beautiful his bride would surely be.

Elsewhere, Mr. Ian Roby had arrived in San Antonio and was reunited with his longtime friend, Hal, for the big golf day they had been looking forward to for months. He thought about the last time he had golfed there in Paris with Lance and hoped he was not rusty.

Before leaving Hallettsville to meet Hal, he met with Dez and Eli at their house for a second time. The two of them came up with a song for Lance and Valtora. Ian liked the lyrics so much that he asked Dez to write one for him to sing to Vantora one day. After telling Dez of his and Vantora's comical experiences and the serious talks with each other, Dez already had in mind how she would write his song.

While waiting for Hal to get in from work, Ian Roby called Vantora in Paris and had a lengthy conversation with her. It was strange for the both of them, so far away. They spoke about the trip to Madrid, and set the time and date to be there before Valtora's wedding in the Spring.

She mentioned that Tory and a few of his friends were really looking forward to the trip. Ian told her that he wanted to consider his vacation to Spain just that, a *vacation*, and no singing engagements. So, she agreed, but added, "And if I wanted a private audience to hear you sing, may I request the song you sang when you came off the stage that night?"

"I'd be delighted," he said. And she could hear him smiling through the phone.

Ian had enjoyed the visit with his mother and sister, Michelle. He even had a few words to shed light on her dilemma about that unsolved case. Because Michelle had taken his advice, things turned out well. Within a day, things worked out.

Antonio had a long, confidential, off-the-record conversation with Michelle in a way that preserved the doctor-patient relationship, even in light of the fact that Antonio treated his father for a condition that was eventually known to be Alzheimer's and needed to be under his professional care. During such care, Brant told him everything...what had happened to the Internet Café person who had moved away, along with the information about Kevin pursuing Brant's idea of retaliating. While in that doctor's office setting, Antonio told his father that he did not need to hear any more, that he had heard enough. The main thing now was for him to treat his father as a patient and take good care of him.

Officer Roby respected his position and considered that particular case, *the first time for everything*, namely, the first unsolved case that would stay unsolved for her.

Antonio went to Austin, Texas and took Kevin up on his offer to take a look at his place and all that came with it. It was the first of several trips his assistant had placed on his travel itinerary. In two weeks Antonio would attend the Medical Seminar to be held in Connecticut. He would go as a replacement to the original invitee, a colleague of his from the Cranbrook Institution in Yoakum, Texas.

The approach to the city limits of Austin had a very different appearance to Antonio's day-to-day entrance into Hallettsville. With the directions that his new assistant had printed out for him in hand (which included extra little landmarks that showed his assistant's familiarity with the area), Antonio smiled and thought to himself as he passed the billboard advertising the beautiful Lake Travis, *"this venture to find Kevin is going to be a piece of cake."*

With the thought of cake, his hunger blared as if a siren went off in his stomach. He made a detour to a restaurant, convincing himself that he would not go to Kevin's work place and eat in that cafeteria. He figured Kevin would understand his decision. After all, he too was a doctor and no doubt welcomed a meal away from the hospital where he worked.

After his delightful meal, he continued on to the Travis County Hospital where Kevin practiced medicine as one of the psychologists on duty. On his route, just as shown on the directions, he saw located on I-35 North the newly constructed Wes Haley Hotel, the first of its brand name to be constructed in Texas. It would only be another twenty miles now after he turned onto Farm to Market Road 4370. He now saw the name of the town Kevin told him. It was called Lake Way.

As Antonio got closer to Lake Way and made it to the top of one of the hills, he noticed that the lake took on the appearance of the winding highway he had been traveling for some time now. He pulled over to the scenic outlook area, got out, and gazed upon the beauty of the winding lake. It was picture perfect with its beautiful blue water. How it went on and on amazed him. He saw sailboats galore and thought as he nodded very slowly, *Kevin has done well for himself, what a great area to live!* He stretched his back and arms as if trying to touch the sky and then glanced at his watch, which if it could talk would have said, *I know you wish you could stay and take in this moment longer, but…*so he returned to his car and continued once he had located the directions.

True once again to his assistant's precision, Antonio was in the parking lot of the Travis County Hospital. *"Now if I can read the directory, I should be able to take it from here,"* he said aloud as he placed the directions into the glove compartment.

He entered the hospital, and there on the wall beside the elevator was the hospital's directory. Skimming quickly down to Psychology, he found Kevin Stanley. "Okay, fifteenth floor," he said in an undertone.

The elevator smelled of recently used wood polish. It was comfortable - elegant almost, with wall and ceiling panels placed strategically between long, perfect mirrors, and marble-like flooring that appeared to have just been waxed and buffed. Its movement was almost undetectable and arrived at its destination quickly.

After he arrived at the fifteenth floor and as soon as the elevator doors opened, there, in the distance, through the interior glass doors, he saw Kevin talking to a couple. He went to the receptionist and told her that Kevin Stanley was expecting him.

After buzzing Kevin's office, she said to Antonio, "Make yourself comfortable. There's coffee and cold drinks in the lounge refrigerator. Doctor Stanley will be with you after his session with his clients."

"Thank you very much," said Antonio, bowing slightly as he turned to follow her directions. He entered the lounge and repeated the receptionist's words, 'Dr. Stanley will be with you...' He shook his head, reached for the coffee pot, and thought to himself "*Dr. Stanley! My my, Kevin has certainly changed – just as he said he had. Definitely not the Kevin I knew in college.*"

"It couldn't have been more perfect timing!" Kevin exclaimed enthusiastically as he appeared at the door with a wide grin and outstretched arms.

"Hey, Kevin, I mean, Dr. Stanley!" Antonio put his coffee down and reached for his friend's hand.

As they shook hands and embraced, each was sincerely happy to see the other.

Long and slow, Kevin said, "Tony, Tony, Tony."

BEYOND ENCOUNTERS

CHAPTER EIGHT

With Paris' peak vacation season ended and winter almost at its end, Valtora decided it was time to get back to the United States with her varied interests there, namely, family in Texas and her fiancé in New York. *Wedding plans, arrangements, and the whole ball of wax,* she thought as she geared up to inform the Hotel staff. *And what a wonderful ball of wax*! She cupped her teary eyes in her hands as she realized how things were about to change for her.

It would be the way she and Van had spoken about so many times while growing up sharing the same bedroom. Valtora's conversations centered on getting married, cooking for her husband as she so many times watched her mother do for their dad, having children, and all of the motherly things she looked forward to.

Once, at age eight, her mother allowed her to cook dinner for the family. The understanding was that Valtora would cook, Mom would assist only if needed, and Vantora would wash dishes and clean the kitchen. Everyone was happy with their assignment before the assignment began.

There Valtora stood; mentally ready to get dinner underway. Her mother even allowed her to decide what the dinner would consist of. The favorite dish that Valtora knew would make her dad happy was the wonderful meatloaf dinner she had watched her mother prepare many times over the years.

She located and set out all necessary items to accomplish what turned out to be the beginning of her cooking career. Little did she know that this meal was preparing her for a future with a restaurant owner. *My very first meal* she thought. *I hope it turns out even better than Mom's.*

As her mother watched, her smile never disappeared during the whole cooking tutorial. However, there was one who's facial expression did change from excitement to total bewilderment, bafflement, puzzlement, and almost panic. It was Vantora. It seemed Valtora went overboard in the use of bowls, cooking utensils, pans, even skillets. Not to mention measuring cups, measuring spoons, even items Vantora did not even know existed in the kitchen cabinets, and which she was almost certain

Valtora just discovered.

Why doesn't she do like Mom and just use her hands for a lot of that stuff she's measuring or her fingers to measure a pinch? Who has ever heard of measuring salt in a measuring spoon and then putting the measured amount in a holding cup? And why does she have to use a separate cutting board for onions and bell pepper? Couldn't she just crack those eggs right over the ground chuck? Oh, but no, she has to beat them in a separate container. "Mom!" cried Vantora, "Does Val have to use *so* many dishes? I'll be washing them until *morning*," Van whined further to her mother.

It was quite amusing to Mrs. Kessley. She was amused not only by Valtora's serious expressions in cooking dinner, but now at Vantora's complaining. It would be a memorable scene for years to come and long after the girls left home and had families of their own.

When it was time for Valtora to leave, the staff at Paris Sofitel Arc de Triomphe Hotel all but had her sign a contract stating she would return each peak season to care for the tourists, even though she would then be the newly married, Mrs. Valtora *Haggerty*. She as much as agreed because she and Lance had discussed such a thing before he moved out of Paris, especially since his father, Leonard Haggerty remained there. A yearly visit for an extended three month stay would be good, although Lance himself would travel back and forth during those three months to his job at the Firm as well as tend to his restaurant.

Lance felt he would have a word with his nephew, Tory, about a conversation regarding his culinary courses after exhausting his scholarship at NYU. Tory would need tuition money and Lance envisioned him taking care of his own restaurant while he and Valtora visited Paris. He recognized Tory as a very responsible young man.

Spring announced its arrival as the Texas landscape began to explode with the appearance of the Bluebonnets. At times, depending on where one happened to be in Texas, the Indian Blankets bloom just before the Bluebonnets. Then the pink Buttercup flowers join the beautiful scene that unfolds and is captured by the families that have once again made their way to what has become a landmark known as, the Rolling Bluebonnet Hills, located on Brant's property.

It served as the perfect location for outdoor weddings, graduation shots and picture-book photos for tourists who happened upon it every year.

Between the picturesque views of her grandparents flower laden field and her parent's bountiful large white spider lilies that surrounded the front yard's cottonwood trees, Adreanna was at a dilemma as to where she would have her wedding when the time came for it. Her storybook wedding, as she had told her mother so many times, would originate from the mobile home on their property, from which she and all in her wedding party would descend the stairs from the porch between the huge cedars and onto the long sidewalk where the plush monkey grass lined each side, winding its way to the white-columned front circular porch, where she, as the bride, and her groom would stand. It was the wedding she imagined since as far back as she could remember.

As she grew older, however, Adreanna's preferences changed. It would be an island wedding, directly on the beach she thought... yes, on the beach, barefooted. Her groom, whoever it would be, would want the same thing, to take her away to white sandy beaches and sun and waves. The beach is where her heart has always been, and she was sure it would be just that way. When she heard about her Uncle Lance's upcoming wedding, she was eager to know how Valtora would plan it. All in all, Adreanna would get all the ideas she needed from her uncle's wedding and would use only what went along with her childhood wedding dreams.

Valtora's wedding day was soon approaching, as sure as the morning comes. Anticipation on their part was enhanced by the return of the beautiful ensemble of spring flowers.

Valtora mentioned to Van that she liked Adreanna and enjoyed her company when she went with her to New York. Additionally, Val said, "You know, I would like for Adreanna to be in our wedding. Do you think she'd mind being in her Uncle's wedding?"

"I think she would love being in it. Good idea," Van replied.

"Well, I'll talk it over with Lance and perhaps he has someone in mind for her to march with."

"Sounds good. And me, who will I march with?"

"Well, Lance says there's this two-left-footed guy at his office that never gets invited to anything, and if you didn't mind, he'd bring him down to march with you."

"You're kidding me, right?" She wasn't amused.

"Wow! That sounds like a no? Should I tell Lance you'll decline his considerate gesture?"

"Well, duh. I can think of a whole lot of other guys I'd rather march with, but I'd narrow the list down to one...Ian. Remember Ian Roby? You know, the guy your hotel engaged for that magnificent singing? How soon some people forget."

"Oh, I didn't forget, I was just thinking of calling in one of those favors I so graciously extended to you not so very long ago. The most recent one where I allowed a certain little sister to accompany me to New York...that's the one I had in mind." She smiled wildly.

"Oh no, not now, not for your wedding. Well, now that I think about it, it is your wedding after all. But don't ask me to wear my shoes on the wrong feet, because that'll be going too far."

At this point Valtora was beside herself with laughter but decided to let Van hold the thought of walking with this imaginary character for a little while longer before she told her that she would indeed walk with Ian in her wedding.

* * *

In an effort to get better acquainted with the woman that would become her Aunt, Dez thought she would offer a bit more information and hoped it would be helpful, especially since Valtora had just arrived and had only now begun preparation for her wedding.

During the course of a conversation Dez had with Mr. Roby, she learned that his mother, Ina was a seamstress.

Dez couldn't wait to speak to Valtora, so she called her as soon as she thought Val would be home to tell her about Ina Roby's line of work.

"Seems we'll all be family soon, Valtora. Congratulation on your upcoming marriage to Uncle Lance," said Dez after Valtora answered the phone.

"I must tell you, we didn't do a poem for him to recite to you if you had said "No" to his proposal. He was really hoping you'd say yes, and when you did, well, you know the rest."

"It was such a sweet poem, Dez," said Valtora. "Thank you for doing it for us."

"It was fun writing it. Valtora, I was calling to see if there's anything I can do to help with your wedding. I'd love to help out."

"Well, I spoke with Lance today about having Adreanna in our wedding and he's happy about it if you - and of course Adreanna - like the idea."

"Oh, I'm sure Adreanna will be thrilled. I'll help her with the accessories... although, she knew what she wanted to wear with what when she went into Kindergarten. Now your dress...what about your dress? Have you gotten it?"

Immediately Valtora put her hand on the top of her head and exclaimed, "My wedding dress! I was supposed to get fitted when I got to New York! But then with looking at rings and going here and there with the overly talkative realtor, it totally, I mean totally slipped my mind."

"That's understandable Valtora."

"Dez, promise me one thing."

"What might that be?"

"Please promise not to call me Aunt Valtora. 'Val' will do."

"Easy enough - Val it is. Now Val, I think you know Ian's mother is here, right?"

"Yes, I was told as I stepped off the plane," she joked.

"Did you know she's a seamstress?"

"No, I didn't. Ian didn't mention it. He did tell me that she made the best butter pound cakes, ever! ..And that she shares them with anyone who would order them, but as far as being a seamstress, no, I didn't know that."

"Men!" Dez exclaimed. "They sure know about the food and the desserts. Eli loves his mother's pecan pies. And he has another source of sweets now that we've found my mother, Suzanna LeAnn. She makes the best chocolate chip cookies from a recipe Mrs. Johnston gave her. She's a lady who visited someone next door to my mother when she was in the Cranbrook Institution in Yoakum."

"I see. I was so happy when Lance told me what had happened," said Valtora. "He also told me you might write about it all... in a book."

"Yes, I've already begun writing. In fact, since there's so much to tell about, and now Uncle Lance's and your wedding, well, I'm thinking of making it a trilogy. Do you think it would get out there?"

"Oh yes, Dez, what has happened in your family happens in more families than we know. It's just that some don't turn out the way yours has. And writing about it just might help others to be happy for those who do eventually get reunited. I think you should continue it and the trilogy idea sounds very good," said Valtora.

"Well thank you. Val, my reason for calling was to help you, and now look, you've been encouraging me."

"You've been very helpful, Dez. And I'll speak directly with Mrs. Roby to see if she's up to tailoring my wedding dress. Thank you for that information!"

"Just let me know however I can help," pleaded Dez.

"I most definitely will," Val promised as they said their good-byes.

BEYOND ENCOUNTERS

CHAPTER NINE

"Val?" asked Van, "Can you believe that '*this day*' that you and I used to talk about while sitting on our twin beds is finally here?"

"I know!" Val exclaimed, "I only wish it were a double wedding, yours and mine."

"For the first time in my life, Val, my mind isn't on what I used to tell you. I remember saying that I wanted to travel and see the world, but I think I've seen enough now...So, if some nice young man asked me to pursue a relationship with marriage in mind, I think I'm ready." She paused. "No, I know for a certainty that I'm ready. You know, Val, it doesn't seem that long ago when Lance was at the Internet Café putting your contact numbers in his palm pilot, and you were very vague about him when I started asking questions about the two of you, remember?"

"Yes, I remember. I hurried out the door to avoid all the questions that were sure to come...from my *little sister*," said Val. "I was the first to be delivered you know."

"Yes, a fact that you'll never forget, nor will you allow me to," Van said as she slowly shook her head.

"Well, are you ready for your wedding? I'm sure Lance is ready to get married."

"Yes, I'm ready to get married."

"Ian should be here tomorrow," said Van with a blushing tone.

"How did I know that we weren't going to end our sister to sister chat without hearing that name Ian?" asked Val, as she used her fingers to put quotation marks to his name.

"Well, I would think that you, of all people, would be happy...well, maybe not just you," Van said as she interrupted herself. "Let me rephrase that. I'd think you and Mom, of all people, would be happy that my focus in life has changed. This is exactly what the two of you wanted for my future... and yes, I'm hoping Ian will be in it."

"Oh, sweetie, I'm speaking for myself, and I'm so happy priorities have made a shuffle in your life towards sharing it with a special man, and hopefully this one who picked you up from the restroom floor at that hotel in

Paris will be the one. Then you won't have to share that little embarrassing tidbit with anyone else, seeing how it *was* Ian who came to your rescue."

"You know what Val?" asked Van. She could not prevent the smile that crossed her face nor the little girly giggle that followed, "I haven't told anyone what I'm about to tell you...I told Mom about that embarrassing incident in Paris... but, not this."

"Oh my, a secret! We haven't shared secrets since, wow! I don't know when the last time was," exclaimed Val. "Tell me! Tell me! What is it? I really want to know!"

"You'd think I had enough of falling, literally falling head over heels for Ian. Well, I have to tell you about *the* most embarrassing moment I have ever had in my entire life."

"The most embarrassing moment in your *whole* life, Van? Come on, what could be more embarrassing than falling in the men's restroom and to the floor at the feet of the man you had only just met on the plane earlier that same day?"

"Had there been just one other guy in there with him and doing 'you know what' at the horse trough, this embarrassment I'm going to tell you about now wouldn't have been so bad."

"Oh my goodness, tell me, Van!" shouted Val.

"Okay, okay already. While you were in New York looking at apartments with Lance, Ian made a quick visit here to see his mother and sister for the second time. On this particular trip, he met Mom and Dad."

"Wow, I've had wedding on the brain, I had no idea he made a second trip here."

"Wedding? No, I think, 'Lance' would be a better choice of words to describe what's been on your brain."

"Yeah, yeah, I'm all ears now so keep talking," she said.

"So, after meeting Mom and Dad, Dad had to go to his office. Then, Mom went to the store to pick up Ian's favorite ice cream, butter pecan. You know Mom; she'll accommodate anyone who walks through our door with that southern hospitality of hers.

Ian and I were sitting right here in this very spot. He asked me to show him the meal that I said I had made the night before, to prove to him that I could cook. So here I went, and as soon as I stepped into the kitchen, I slipped and hit the floor so hard. I mean I fell on my rump so hard! I was more embarrassed about falling than feeling the hurt I vaguely knew was there."

Laughing without letup, Val managed to get out, "What did you do then?"

"If you stop laughing, I'll tell you."

"Okay, okay, I'm done, so tell me what you did; I mean what did Ian do?"

"I just lay there on my left side with my face buried in my hands and groaned as if I were more hurt than embarrassed."

"What did *he* do?"

"He hurried over to me, and as he asked me if I was alright, he was holding his hands out for me to grab. He said, "Let me help you up." I raised my hand and he took it and helped me to my feet. He then said, "You truly are falling for me, aren't you?" Then he hugged me and patted me on my back. I couldn't believe I had fallen again right before his very eyes, and what's so bad about it was, I was trying to impress him with my cooking."

"Van, that must have been *the* most embarrassing moment in your life. So other than that, how was his visit?"

"Well, I had anticipated his coming over the night before, and knew from meeting him on the plane and spending time with him in Paris, that he had a clown side, kind of playful and all. So....."

"Uh oh, what did you do in anticipation of his visit? Because we are twins *and* the fact that I know you so well, all of this is telling me that you were doing more conniving than anticipating."

"Then I guess it's true what people say about twins being on the same wavelength. That's a good *and* bad thing," said Van.

"Now tell me what were you going to say after that 'so'....," said Val.

"I had bought a Frisbee, and one of those bubble guns that make tiny bubbles when you wave it around, and two water guns, a purple one and an orange one.

Okay, so the night before he came to the house, I took both of them out of their packages, filled the orange water gun with water, then stapled both of them back in their packages... you know, just as I had bought them. When he came over, I told him I bought all these toys."

"Wait, wait. How old are you? I mean how old are we?"

Van started laughing, more about what happened with Ian that day than the funny look on Val's face as she asked those questions.

"Anyway," said Van, ignoring her, "I asked him if he would spray me with the water gun that he was holding if it had water in it." He said, 'You better believe I would.' I asked him, 'Really? You mean you'd spray me?' He rolled his eyes to the ceiling and restated more emphatically, 'Absolutely!' So, at that point we both opened our packages that I had so neatly stapled back, and as he sat there looking at his purple one like he was inspecting it for shipment to Toys R Us, I pointed mine at him and started spraying it right in his face and in his hair, and on his neck. Val, he was totally shocked and said, 'No, you didn't just spray me. You launched a surprise attack on me.' Then I said, 'Uh oh.' and I gave him a towel."

"Did he take it well?" asked Val.

"If you call his getting up and going to the kitchen where I had only ten minutes ago fallen, and then filling up his water gun mumbling something all the while he was filling it up, and then totally soaking me, even chasing me all over the place "taking it well" ..then I'd say he was probably annoyed, only just a little. But we laughed so hard during the whole episode, especially when I got a pillow for a shield. It was Mom's favorite, the one with the fringes. It got even funnier because I was able to avoid his marksmanship of shots that barreled in directly to my face. I got him good. It was totally fun with him. I hated to see him go."

"Yep, the two of you have been bitten by the love bug. Others see it before the two involved do. That's usually how it is," said Val.

Mrs. Kessley tapped on the girls' door and made them aware that they were going to miss the early morning bride's breakfast if they did not get some sleep. They agreed and as quietness filled the room their parents talked about the upcoming marriage of their daughter.

Mr. Roby arrived in Hallettsville with more than enough time to visit Vantora. He used the opportunity before the wedding to recite the edited poem Dez gave him from her collection of poems and songs, the one meant originally for Lance and Valtora. Ian and Vantora went to the City Park, and there as he looked intently at her, he spoke the words of the poem:

Your Eyes to Mine

My imagination has found your eyes to mine
I have longed for the time when we would bind
The most intense happiness I have ever ever known,
Stares in my direction, yes, Van, our love is full blown
Allow what's mutual between us to grow, let it live,
There's no reason with me to be apprehensive,

Don't hold back no don't you furl
As you place your eyes to mine, oh baby girl,
Your eyes to mine (is what I want, so) please,
Look in my direction the way you know how
Let's make our love last and soon we'll endow
Each other with the reality of the imagined
Yes, Van, I want your eyes to mine

Entreat me more and more not to lose our intent
This gaze as we lock this most precious moment.
Never let go of your eyes to mine oh no no no
I love you so…believe me when I say,
My eyes are on you, to you, for you, with you,

Let's just gaze and see what the future could hold
I promise to keep you warm yes you'll never be cold
I want to share these feelings that I have about you
Will you please marry me and say I do

Van was touched by the sincere tone of Ian's voice as he lovingly spoke the words to her. She was even more touched when he took hold of her left hand, drew her close, and with her eyes looking into his, he asked her if she would marry him.

"Yes! Yes, I will, Ian Roby!" she answered with sheer delight.

She blinked her tear-filled eyes a few times to clear her vision as Ian brought forth out of his pocket a small white leather case that held the engagement ring. After placing it on her finger, they left to prepare for her sister's wedding.

Van and Ian had a great opportunity to spend time together that evening, mainly because the biggest event in her sister's life was the next day. She and Ian both felt that this *"perhaps something"* that developed between the two of them while in Paris, was *"truly something"* indeed.

They agreed to inform every one of their engagement after her sister's wedding.

During the reception, Ian held to his promise to Valtora and sang for them, the newly wedded couple. Valtora watched her sister as he sang and knew just from how Vantora looked at him that it would not be long before the two of them would have their wedding day.

The song Ian and Dez compiled was called *Amazing*.

AMAZING

From deep within my soul I found you there
I found what I've been looking for and it's rare
It's a find, yes, a find for which I want to care
For a long long time and to all I will declare

That my love for you is simply amazing
I tell you dear, it's just simply amazing, oh
My it's so incredible how this love of mine
For you is tantalizing to the core of my heart and

The point of it all is the feeling is mutual I feel
When you say the things you say to me I reel
In a way that I never knew before oh and the thrill
Fills my soul to the point that I can only know and say

That my love for you is simply amazing

I tell you dear, it's just simply amazing, oh
My it's so incredible how this love of mine
For you is tantalizing to the core of my heart and

It's our world that we've come to have and a
Togetherness that anyone will rightly say
Belongs to you and me my love, yes you and me
My sweet love together we are simply amazing and know

That my love for you is simply amazing
I tell you dear, it's just simply amazing, oh
My it's so incredible how this love of mine
For you is tantalizing to the core of my heart and it's

Amazing...

Once again Valtora parted the crowd, but this time she was holding onto the arm of Lance. They left the crowd to board the plane for Paris as Van and their mother looked on in tears.

Gifts to the bridesmaids from Valtora were small personalized picture albums, with the first photo being one of her and Lance. Val also gave them a diary to match the album. All the girls were happy to get the useful gifts from Val. Each one immediately began writing down their private thoughts, as well as the things that had captured a place in their hearts that they did not want to soon pass from their memory.

BEYOND ENCOUNTERS

CHAPTER TEN

Suzanna's meditation as she sat in the porch swing this particular morning was interrupted by an unfamiliar car in the distance driving up to the house. It did not turn away at the "Y". As it got closer, pulling into the driveway, she discerned that it had two strange men inside. A man got out of the car and slowly walked up to the front porch. His voice was gentle as he spoke to Suzanna, "In town, at the Internet Café, I was told that Brant Chamberlain could be found here. Does he live here?"

"Who are you and why are you looking for Brant Chamberlain?"

"I'm sorry ma'am; I do apologize for not introducing myself. I'm Evan Kinkaid. My father knew Brant's mother, Candace Chamberlain... in France. Before he died he gave me something that I was to give to Brant when I made it to the States. Actually... he died a few months ago, so I'm here now to care for some of his interests. I've been here in the States for several weeks but only now have I had the opportunity to travel the distance from New York to take care of what I promised my father. I won't rest easy until I have given it to him."

"How long will you be here?" asked Suzanna.

"Until evening tomorrow, then I must get back to New York and tend to my father's interests there."

"May I have a number where you can be reached? I'll see to it that Brant gets your message. You can expect to hear from him."

"Yes, here's my card. And thank you. Have a good day." He tipped an imaginary hat and turned to walk away.

"Thank you," Suzanna replied quietly, gazing at the card.

The men left as peacefully as they had arrived. Suzanna had a strange feeling about the incident, but nevertheless chose to inform Brant after he and Arthur returned from Eli's feed store. She was determined not to ask the questions that she had wanted to ask for so long, although now, with this mysterious man's inquiry about her husband, those questions nagged at her even more. *Who is this Evan Kinkaid,* she thought, *He says he has something from his father to give to Brant, but why has he really come? Will what he has for Brant be detrimental to him? Why does this have to happen now, so soon after we've gotten back together?*

Suzanna had more questions she was about to hurl at herself, but the telephone rang. She got up from the porch swing to answer, and it was Alice calling from Seattle to get her routine 'once a month' report about how everyone was doing. It took all of an hour for the question and answer session to wind down before the two of them began to talk about each other's welfare.

After exchanging how both were fairing, Suzanna always managed to get into their conversation the phrase, "Alice, you shouldn't be alone." Have you even turned your head to the right or to the left? Now you do know there's only a very slim chance of him standing right in your path."

With a kidding lilt in her voice, Alice replied as she always did, "What took you so long to ask me about getting married again *this* time Suzi? You're getting a little bit slow there, aren't you?"

"I'm so happy with Brant, Alice! I just want you to have someone other than the children to share your life with."

"I know you care, Suzi. I haven't, in all the years following Eli's father's death, met anyone that could fill that man's shoes. I haven't been looking. Even if I were interested, Suzi, I don't think it would be fair to him."

"Fair to him?" asked Suzanna.

"Yes, to the man I would be interested in sharing my life with." At that point Alice broke down and wept. She could not continue.

"Alice, I didn't mean to make you cry. Are you thinking of the husband you lost?"

After a long pause, Alice said, "I think of him often, Suzi. But, I must tell someone, no, not just anyone. I want to tell you."

"Tell me what, Alice? I think you *need* to talk to me. Please take your time. I'm here for you."

"For some time I haven't been feeling well. I feel something is terribly wrong and I can only imagine the worst."

"You have gone to the doctor, haven't you, Alice?"

"Yes, I did. He ran tests and told me I should come in so he could talk with me about the results, and that my suspicions about something being wrong were correct. I told him I wanted to make my grandchildren's graduation in Texas, and then I would come in to discuss his findings. As of yet I haven't gone, but I know it's time to see after myself. With this looming over me, and I know you mean well, Suzi, I simply cannot burden a mate with what may be a serious health condition. It wouldn't be fair."

"Eli? What about Eli? You haven't told him, have

you?"

"No, I haven't. I was planning to talk with him the next time I visited."

"Well, I tell you the truth Alice, you're not scheduled to come here for a while, so I'm telling you out of the utmost concern, come now! Call Eli and tell him you want to come sooner. I know you want to see the children and all, so come on and talk with Eli and Dez. Dez loves you like a mother. She has told me many times how close the two of you have become over the years. So tell me now, Alice, you will be here soon."

"Yes, I will, Suzi."

"Promise?"

"Yes," said Alice, "I promise."

"Okay, and when you get here, *after* you talk with the children, you and I can spend a little time together. I say 'little' because knowing Dez, you won't be here long. She'll have you on that plane going back to Seattle to the doctor. So be prepared *not* to stay the two months."

"I think you're absolutely right. In fact, I'll pack light this time."

"Good idea. I'll be thinking about you, Alice, and try not to worry dear. Now I understand that there's more to it than you just telling me you can't find that *someone* to fill your late husband's shoes. I love you, Alice. We all love you, and we're all here to support you no matter what the results. So you be strong."

"Thank you, Suzi, I appreciate your encouragement! I'm so glad Brant found you. He found you not only for his and his children's sake, but also for the sake of all those whose lives touch yours, and I'm so grateful that mine did. I feel optimistic now, regardless of any negative findings."

"Alice, you give me too much credit. I can't take credit for what should go to the One who inspires me to feel the way I feel, to do the things I do and to say the things I say. Through it all, in my case, a higher source helped me cope with what life has brought my way, and that same divine source continues to guide me. So we both can thank our Maker, the One who deserves all the praise."

"I agree, Suzi, and I love you for being the way you are. What a beautiful friend has come into my life! Let me let you go now. We've never talked so long over the telephone. Please give my regards to Brant. I'll give you a call when I get there. Take care."

"I'll be looking forward to seeing you, Alice, goodbye."

Suzanna felt a sudden pull. She followed it and found herself in the kitchen, rummaging through the cabinets to bake her famous chocolate chip cookies. She recollected the ones she had made for Jake and Tory, and at the thought of it she almost could smell the aroma drifting by her nose. She also called to mind how she came about obtaining the recipe for the *great tasting* cookies, so termed by her grandchildren. She had gotten it from a visitor to the Cranbrook Institution when she was a patient there.

*

A former doctor, who had taken a leave of absence from her practice to recuperate from fatigue, occupied the room next to Suzanna LeAnn at the Cranbrook Institution in Yoakum. She had a frequent visitor by the name of Billie Mae Johnston, of Hallettsville.

Mrs. Johnston had a husband, Leroy Johnston, and he was the Limousine Cattle rancher from whom Brant had bought his cattle when he first arrived in Hallettsville. Because Suzanna had already met Billie, when it became public who Brant was in relation to Suzanna, all that could be said was "it's a small world!"

Mrs. Billie Johnston brought a special type of chocolate chip cookie to her friend on numerous occasions during Suzanna's stay. The doctor always wanted Mrs. Johnston to drop some off to Suzanna. During one of her stops, Suzanna asked Mrs. Johnston for the recipe to those cookies.

Mrs. Johnston could not take credit for the recipe and so informed Suzanna, "I'd love to take credit for how delicious the cookies taste, but the recipe was my mother's, Christine Repschleger. She had gotten the recipe from *her* mother. So it's been around for a long time. And sure, you may have it. Your neighbor, Dr. Boller, told me that you'll be leaving on Wednesday. Soon you'll be able to bake some for your family."

"What's the secret ingredient that makes them so different from all the other chocolate chip cookies I've tasted?" asked Suzanna.

"Since it's a special recipe and the walls may be listening, I'll just write it down for you and you'll notice the 'what' that makes them so different," answered Mrs. Johnston, with a smile.

With that, Mrs. Johnston, because she had made them often, wrote by heart the recipe for Suzanna:

Preheat oven at 375 degrees

1 heaping cup brown sugar

1 cup white sugar

2 sticks oleo

2 teaspoons vanilla

1 teaspoon butter extract

1 ½ teaspoon almond extract

3 eggs (beat well)

3 cups flour

1 teaspoon baking soda

1 teaspoon salt

2 cups pecans (chopped)

1 ½ cups chocolate chips

Combine sugars, oleo, and flavorings, beat until creamy. Add in beaten eggs. In a separate bowl combine: flour, soda, and salt. Gradually add combined dry ingredients into creamy mixture until gone. Then add in pecans and chocolate chips. Drop by well-rounded teaspoons onto non greased cookie sheet. Bake 10 to 12 minutes

"Oh, thank you Mrs. Johnston!" Suzanna said, clearly delighted. I'm sure you have other recipes tucked away in your recipe box. Perhaps after I'm settled in at my own home, you'll share more of your recipes. I'm also looking forward to making special dinners for my husband, Brant. You should publish a dessert cookbook and include a section on the other special recipes of Mrs.

Repschleger's that I know you must have," said Suzanna.

"Sure, I'll be happy to share my recipes. Publishing them has crossed my mind lots of times, Suzanna, and you just may have talked me into actually doing it. Thank you for that," said Mrs. Johnston. "By the way, you say your husband is Brant? Is that Brant Chamberlain?"

"Yes, do you know him?" asked Suzanna.

"Yes, he bought quite a few head of cattle from my husband some years back. So he'll know exactly where to bring you for your first visit to our house."

"That sounds fine, Mrs. Johnston. I can't wait to get out of here and do for Brant after so long being apart."

"Please, call me Billie. I'm so happy for you Suzanna," said Mrs. Johnston as she reached inside her purse and gave her a small wrapped present.

"Oh, how sweet of you!" said Suzanna. "Thank you."

"Well, I'll be going now. You take care of yourself and I'm looking forward to your visit to our home."

At that point Suzanna went to her dresser and looked at what Mrs. Johnston had gotten for her as a departing gift from Cranbrook. She brushed a lone tear from her cheek as she looked at her own reflection in the small, gold-trimmed hand mirror Mrs. Johnston had given her.

There was a soft breeze that came in through the window, drying her cheek. After reminiscing for a few minutes, Suzanna continued where she had left off in baking the *great tasting* cookies, before her mind wandered back to her stay at Cranbrook.

She set Mr. Kinkaid's card on the window sill just above the kitchen sink, leaning it up against her favorite figurine in order not to forget to give it to Brant.

*

After Alice finished talking on the phone with Suzanna, she went into her kitchen to bake her famous pecan pie. She thought of how much Eli liked them. She also thought about her imminent visit to Hallettsville to her son's country home. She looked forward to the sunlit back room and the early morning scene that gradually appeared each morning during her extended stays.

BEYOND ENCOUNTERS

CHAPTER ELEVEN

Eli and Dez were central in the lives of Brant and
Suzanna. Suzanna could not make up all of those forty
two years without them fast enough. She and Dez spent a
lot of time together now. They created appointments to be
able to spend as much time on those occasions as possible.

Brant understood perfectly her need to recapture
the time lost between them and so did not mind the occasions she was away. That, coupled with what he had more
recently been thinking about made Brant happy that he
could have this time alone to figure out just what went on
all those years ago when he was so young.

Memories from his childhood continually demanded attention, and now, with Suzanna and his children back in his life, he felt safe. Now he could finally allow himself to revisit those memories, deal with the feelings they brought along with them and expend the emotional time and energy required to evaluate, classify and dismiss them if necessary.

The last time he chose to bring thoughts like these to the surface was when he was the security guard at the Grande Arch de la Defense Hotel in Paris. The reason for the resurgence of past thoughts was due to the appearance of a snake crossing his path as if from out of nowhere, as he trimmed the edges of the sidewalks.

In that moment he vividly recalled the conversation he had with that man in the living room of their house there in Paris. He was only a small boy, and the man had seen him, although he had no idea at the time. He had certainly spotted Brant while he was hiding behind the sofa. Brant was five years old. He had not taken off his red baseball cap and the top of it could be seen hovering a bit above the sofa, with his name "Brant" embroidered across the cap.

Brant's mother, Candace, had her back to the sofa and thus was unaware of her little boy hiding behind it. The man told Brant that if he was going to hide, he should be as still as a frozen snake.

The man was not aware of little Brant until after

the majority of the heated conversation between Candace and him had already taken place. He was not quite sure how much or how well little five year old Brant had heard or understood.

The reason for the heated conversation was something Brant thought about and puzzled over during the next several decades.

Brant had the habit of running to hide behind the sofa when callers came to the door. This particular time although now a grown man, Brant remembered something from that day that had been put away until *just* now.

With his finding Suzanna and getting back with his two children, calmness had set in within his mind and made room for what had been there for years. What he remembered was what the man said - and it seemed as if it had just been said.

He recalled the man saying, "The boy should know, Candace! The boy should *know*." At that time he had no interest in trying to connect any meaning to what he heard, but he knew the reference to, 'the boy', was to himself. What did it mean? The man's tone made Brant think that it was something important. What should the boy know was a question he had asked himself over and over as he lay in his little bed, night after night.

When his mother left to go to the kitchen, the man made known to little Brant that he was not hidden well enough. He told Brant that he saw his red cap and the next time, so as not to be seen, he should take his cap off. Brant was so shocked that he had been found out, that he very quickly threw his red cap on the floor next to the man's feet. He then ran to his room and closed the door. He barricaded the door with a small chair and some of his reading books in order to keep the man from coming after him (or so he thought) and finishing that conversation.

Those were the memories that Brant, as a grown man, suppressed at times and at other times he would bring them to the fore, examining them.

He would have an opportunity to bring these thoughts out after Suzanna would tell him of the visit from Evan Kinkaid. Although the man did not tell her what it was his father wanted Brant to have, Suzanna suspected that somehow this was related to the same thing that plagued Brant the night he sent her in to bed so he could remain on the front porch swing alone with his thoughts.

Suzanna never pressured Brant about his past, nor did Brant pressure Suzanna about her past. It was an unspoken understanding in regard to Brant's past, a subject that would not be discussed. He left the door open for Suzanna to come to him if she ever wanted to talk with him about *her* past.

As Suzanna sat on the front porch after Evan and

the other man left, and after talking with Alice on the telephone, she had not realized just how long she had remained there, sitting on the swing, after she returned from baking the chocolate chip cookies. She got wrapped up thinking about not only the visit of those strangers and her conversation with Alice, but also with her own past, times of long ago.

At that point she heard the rooster crow, signaling that time of evening, which brought her out of her mesmerized thoughts. She was pulled from her thoughts of all that was happening and yet *to* happen, just in time to see Brant and his brother, Arthur, coming up the lane. The two of them waved at her as they passed by the house on the way to the barn. A few minutes later she caught sight of her grandson, Arelius, as he also drove slowly down the lane to meet them.

Arelius had seen his grandfather and uncle at his dad's feed store and asked his grandfather if he could come out to his place to help with unloading the feed. It was something that Arelius loved to do with Brant and Uncle Arthur, even though at times he was allowed to completely unload the feed on his own.

It seemed that Arelius was content with staying in Hallettsville working the family business. He and Uncle Antonio had on several occasions, discussed this very thing in conjunction with his leaving Hallettsville to pursue what he liked. It always proved to be that Arelius was already happy doing what he was doing.

Antonio told Arelius that he himself helped with his grandfather's shoe store in England when he was even younger than Arelius. Antonio told him that it was a means to an end for him because he had plans of finding his sister, Dez, in the States.

Antonio often asked him, "So, Arelius, what is it that you are planning to do with your life?"

Arelius always responded, "I want to settle down, have a business of my own, get married, have children and maybe some pets." It was always the same question from Antonio and always the same answer from Arelius.

As Arelius neared his achievements Antonio would, on occasion, ask Arelius if he had found the one that he wanted to settle down with. He had no answer for his uncle for the longest time, but things began to look up for Arelius and his answer to his uncle began to take on a different tone. On one of his trips to New York to visit his brother, Tory, he met Karly, the sister of one of Tory's classmates. They communicated regularly through the mail after their first encounter.

It happened when Arelius went to New York on a four-day winter visit. His mother had gotten things squared away with Uncle Lance about picking him up at the airport and made sure that he would make his connections with Tory. Just short of giving him a curfew, she left most things to the discretion of his Uncle Lance.

Tory anticipated his brother's arrival and made a detailed itinerary for his visit. He wanted to make sure that Arelius met Fran's sister, Karly, who had taken a liking to upstate New York, where the concrete was replaced with beautiful houses with grass, trees, and a familiar country look. Tory thought it would be a very interesting encounter between the two of them, and so did Fran. The two of them commented on how they felt like the parents from long ago who chose their children's marriage mates.

When Karly found out that Arelius was coming for a visit, she was beside herself with countless questions to her sister about him: *How old was he? Was he nice looking like Tory? Was he tall? Did he ski? Did he have a girl friend?* The barrage of questions ceased only when Fran left her presence.

When Arelius arrived at LaGuardia airport, Uncle Lance, Aunt Valtora and his brother were all waiting for him in the baggage claim area.

Fran, Karly, and three of Fran's friends had already been chauffeured to Saranac Lake in upstate New York to secure the accommodations for the group. The plan was for Uncle Lance and the boys to meet them for a bit of skiing, on the bunny slopes. Since Tory had no classes on Friday or Monday, it would be a nice long weekend.

When they got to Saranac Lake and had gotten situated in their rented cabin, Tory called Fran and was ready to get the skiing underway with the greatly anticipated planned meeting of Arelius and Karly.

Before they left, Arelius took an extra look around the cabin, appreciative of its architecture. He committed the view to memory and intended to use many of its characteristics in the home he planned to build back in Texas, perhaps down at The Branch near the stream where he used to fish as a small boy. He thought aloud, "I think I'd like to live in a place like this, Uncle Lance."

"It seems to me, Arelius that you're thinking of moving out on your own." Lance always seemed to know more about a matter than one was comfortable admitting.

"You're not too far off base, Uncle Lance. Moving out on my own yes, but, I couldn't picture myself anywhere else except living in the country. That's where I've always wanted to be. I even know now what kind of house I want." He took another long look, placing it carefully in the corner of his mind.

"Well, it won't be hard to figure what kind that would be," said Tory, "a log house, right?"

Arelius laughed. "Right! I can see it at The Branch now, sitting near the stream, just around the area where, when we were kids, we saw the oil on top of the water and I told Dad about it."

"I remember that," recalled Tory. "I can't believe that no more than two weeks after you showed it to us, the oil company came around talking about drilling on our place, and now we have a couple of oil and gas wells there," said Tory. He glanced at his watch. "Well, we'd better get going before the girls take down the slopes without us."

After arriving at the Lodge and getting suited up, Tory and Arelius made their approach to the *dressed-for-the-occasion* group of girls. Meanwhile, their aunt and uncle watched from the enclosed spectators' section. Tory made the introductions and there was no need to do anything further. What brought Arelius and Karly even closer together, besides her excitement over meeting him, was the fact that the two of them were the best skiers of the bunch. They had occasions to ski on the intermediate and the steep slopes with no hint of fear.

Somehow, during the course of the evening, Arelius got both of Karly's telephone numbers, one to the Condo at Saranac Lake and the other to her home back in the city. Karly later told her sister that Arelius told her frankly that he was no writer, but he hoped they would correspond verbally. She was amused at his suggestion that, if she was a writer, *she* could write him.

To Arelius' surprise, Karly revealed that she wrote poetry. That was something that sparked his interest since his mother also enjoyed writing poetry. He told her of their shared interest, and the more he talked about his mother, the more Karly liked her, sight unseen.

Something else that sparked his interest was how in just one long weekend, the both of them came to find out how similar they were in their likes and dislikes, and also in their views and expectations.

It did not take Karly long to form her opinion about the kind of person Arelius was. When they left up-state New York and returned to their home, Karly wrote a poem about Arelius, especially when she understood that he really did look at himself as just an average guy. From the start, she begged to differ, and differ she did, each time he insisted that he was no one special. The poem Karly wrote was entitled, *It Doesn't Matter.*

IT DOESN'T MATTER

Even when you say you're just like everyone else and
That you're human and there's nothing special about
yourself
It doesn't matter because those words fall on deaf ears
and erode
On ears of one who knows the distinctiveness of your
mode

In response to the praiseworthy heartfelt expressions that
are given
Time and again one would hear from you that you are
just human
In begging to differ contrary to your own opinion you are
inimitable
Yes unique unmatched incomparable and truly a force so
stable

It doesn't matter that you would surmise that you are not
deserving of the praise that in your behalf I raise
There are others who would vouch for the fact
that modesty is a quality that you do not lack

You praise your mother for the way you are for that rea-
son you are my star
To your self-perceived way that you are just like anyone
else I declare that proves to me how special you really
are
You have a way that compels you to allow your real self
to show through and when that's done even more it shows
that you do have that special quality yes you are you

It doesn't matter that on any given occasion
You point out with I must admit well-meant persuasion,
That there's no difference between you and the next guy,
I tell you Arelius Ortello that claim one would deny

Somehow, whenever Uncle Antonio questioned him about prospects of who he would settle down with, Arelius managed to turn the conversation to his uncle's personal life. Antonio evidently did not mind, because each time he ended up talking for a while about his interest in the new female chief of police, Michelle Roby. He told Arelius how he first met her when she had gone to the Yoakum Hospital to check on her mother, and how he went down the hallway looking for her. She had been out of his sight and suddenly she appeared when his back was turned, asking him if he was looking for something. It was a story Antonio could tell any of his children in the future, if those children came from a union with Michelle. Furthermore, it was a story he could tell anyone who would listen, like Arelius, and listen Arelius did in order to divert the conversation away from his own selecting of a marriage mate.

The unexpected encounter with Karly on Saranac Lake gave Arelius something to contribute to their next conversation. Only time would tell. He certainly now had something of interest to share with his mother. He thought, *"The fact that Karly writes poems should surely endear her to my mother."* At the very least, it would certainly break the ice when Karly met his parents, which would be a good thing, since he intended to also tell them how much he already liked her.

BEYOND ENCOUNTERS

CHAPTER TWELVE

Eli and Dez were aware that Adreanna and Arelius would soon leave the nest. They also knew it would not be temporary, like when Arelius went for the skiing weekend with Tory in New York, nor like Adreanna's own short New York stay with her brother.

Dez remembered when Adreanna was a child on the beaches of the Texas Gulf Coast, drawing pictures in the sand, and the times she colored pictures for her and Eli, leaving them on their pillows at night. She remembered other times finding them after Adreanna would slide them under their bedroom door and sometimes taping them to the other side.

Now that Adreanna was a teen-ager, Dez knew that her trip to New York sparked a desire to eventually exhibit her work there in SoHo, New York's Art District.

Adreanna's experience at showing her paintings in her small town gave her a taste of what she hoped her future would bring.

As far as Arelius was concerned, though, he had no intentions of living in New York. It was great to visit, sure... but to live there? Not hardly. He liked the old adage, *'There's no place like home.'* Home to Arelius was not necessarily home with his parents, just some good ole' small town country living.

With these prospects right around the corner, Eli and Dez decided to insert travel plans of their own into their lives. Waiting until such time that the possibility of a romantic rendezvous could actually happen, they made plans to travel in the winter, with hopes of getting snowed in somewhere, preferably in Ruidoso, New Mexico. In just a few weeks they would be off for a snowy adventure, just the two of them. In anticipation of the snow and all that comes with such a phenomenal thing, Dez put pen to paper and wrote a poem she called, *Quiet Nights*:

QUIET NIGHTS

There are no sounds when the snow falls to its previous
layer
Muffled sounds have muted the day's activities and one
can but stare
In amazement of that fluffy white blanket yet so cold to
the touch
Nights are equally hushed as the picturesque view holds
so much

An awesome sight as can be seen by the full moon's early
bright light
With tiny twinkles that make themselves known to the
frolicker's sight
The nights are as quiet as the sound heard from the stars
in the sky
A cold winter's night coupled with that heavy mantle of
cover to vie

The most frigid day of the season one can take note of
with eagerness
To enjoy the feat of what has fallen is not to be looked
upon with duress
Getting snowed in has its memories that will linger
throughout the years
And what fond memories they will be for what they

brought were cheers

Quiet nights have many things to tell when sitting around
the fire
It's all cozy and yet different from the cold but it's each
one's desire
Quiet nights have been around and to speak of them is no
endeavor
There are so many memories of quiet nights that they'd
be told forever

As Dez finished her poem, Adreanna came into the living room and peered over her mother's shoulder, reading it aloud. After she read it, she suggested that she compile all of her poetry that she had written over the years and publish a book of poems, insisting that she use her full name - Dezeray Payton Chamberlain Ortello. They both giggled. They remembered Eli kidding Dez about her accumulation of names since discovering that Brant Chamberlain was her biological father.

Adreanna thought of such a thing as her mother writing because every day Adreanna came across some type of literary work at Hallettsville's Public Library. It was not the first time Dez had received encouragement to do some type of writing.

Eli told Dez what the former Chief of Police, Bob

Lacy, had said about someone writing a book that would tell the story of the mysterious newcomer to Hallettsville, Brant Chamberlain. He said the book should eventually reveal that Brant was Dez's father.

Even before Adreanna mentioned this idea to compile poems, Dez had contemplated this very thing and had begun to like the idea. She told herself that if she heard anyone else speak of her writing before she herself pursued such an undertaking, she would indeed set out to doing just that. But for now, Dez was planning their trip to New Mexico and hoped for that romantic snowed-in rendezvous with Eli.

As the time drew closer for them to leave, Dez phoned Jake, as she was in the habit of doing before they left on any trip, to make sure all was well with his health. She wanted to make sure his food cupboards and freezer were full. She found him well and fully supplied, and when he learned where they were going, he was excited that they would be going to a place that all of them had already visited before - a place he was in no hurry to see again.

He recalled the time they had gone as a family to Ruidoso. All was going good for him until the trip to Sierra Blanca Mountain. It was a trip that he wanted to forget because the altitude was hard on him. Even so, he tried his best to enjoy it. His father, sensing something new, something different in relation to Jake's episodes of pain, told the family that they had better get down the mountain before the snow started.

Jake remembered being very grateful and hugging his father's neck, aware that his dad did it for his benefit. Observing the interchange, Dez smiled at Eli to hold back tears, because when Jake hurt, she hurt with him. Each time Jake had physical pain, Dez hurt in an emotional way for her son. She shared a special bond with him because of his special condition. It brought them very close.

During their telephone conversation, Jake made his mother aware of his relationship with Rachel. "Mother, I wanted you to know that I gave Rachel my class ring. She didn't ask for it. I wanted her to have it so the guys would know we were talking, and so they won't get any ideas about talking to her, like, you know, for a girlfriend."

"Oh, yes, I know, Jake. And so the girls would know also, right?" asked Dez.

Jake thought to himself that somehow, moms always knew these things. The playful way his mother asked that question told him that he had his mother's approval, something he cared very much about.

BEYOND ENCOUNTERS

CHAPTER THIRTEEN

After talking with Jake on the telephone, Dez continued finalizing the plans for the trip.

Finally on her "to do" list she reached,

...call Mother and Daddy.

She looked at the list for a while and thought she would do just that, call her mother and let her know that she and Eli were taking off in a few days.

Suzanna answered the telephone and said, "Hello, you've reached the Chamberlain's residence, may I help you?"

"Mom, its Dez. How are you feeling today?"

"I'm doing just fine, Dez. Is everything alright?

The children, are they all alright?" Suzanna would always think along those lines of family, asking these questions first right away, as she herself was still getting used to the feelings of being back with the man of her life, Brant. After so many years of being apart from each other and now being with him, she felt a bit insecure about what was a reality in her mind. She hoped every day that she was truly living such a reality. Only at times would these feelings surface in her mind, thoughts that something was going to come up and return things to the way they were, without Brant, without Dez and without Antonio and the whole family she had gotten close to. She thought this way, off and on, since Brant and Dez came to her at the Yoakum Cranbrook Institution.

Immediately, Dez put her fears to rest. "Everything is really good, Mother. In fact, things are going so well at this point that Eli and I are going to the mountains for a few days, and I just wanted you and Daddy to know about it." The silence she heard at the other end of the phone concerned her. "Mother, is everything alright?"

"Dezeray, I'm not sure."

"Aren't you feeling well?"

"Oh, I feel fine, Dez, it's just that there was this man..."

Suzanna could not finish what she was going to say before Dezeray, with her own inner feelings about how her mother began the sentence, interrupted.

"Man, what man, Mother? Is he still there? What did he want?"

Suzanna recalled the whole story about Brant's

first encounter with Dez and Eli at the Internet Café, and this was probably surfacing in Dez's mind. So to calm her fears, Suzanna answered her questions slowly saying, "A man from Paris came looking for your father. He said his father knew Brant's mother, and that he had something his father made him promise to hand deliver to Brant. He's gone now, but wants to see Brant before he leaves Hallettsville tomorrow. Your father has just come home and is still outside with Arelius and Arthur."

"I want to come over now if I may, Mother. Please, I would like to be in on this from the very beginning. Too much has happened in our lives for us to allow any more things to come between us. May I?"

"Why sure, honey, I want you to be here when I tell your father about that man."

"Ok, I'll be right there." She had barely hung up the phone before she already had keys in hand.

As Dez was about to turn into her father's driveway, she saw Arelius in Brant's lane coming toward her. She waited for him to come out and as Arelius approached her, he stopped and was curious about why she was heading to his grandfather's house. She simply said that she wanted to visit with her mother before they left for New Mexico. Satisfied as he always was with explanations from his parents, he told his mother that he would see her when she returned home.

When Dez reached her mother's house, Suzanna had gone back to the front porch swing, where the stranger, Evan Kinkaid, found her earlier in the day. Dez went onto the porch and gave her mother a long hug and kissed her on the cheek, "Hello, Mother, I love you." Then she smiled, "Has Dad come to the house yet?"

"No, not yet."

"Well, let's just wait here until he comes before we talk about that man who was here asking for him."

"Okay, that's a good idea, Dez, and I'm so glad you wanted to be here when I told him. We should handle things as a family now and not have any more secrets. We've learned and grown together over time. It's been entirely too much time if you ask me."

"Yes, I agree." Dez said resolutely. "I hope Dad will also feel the same. No matter what it is that the man wants to talk to Dad about, I hope he doesn't feel that it's so bad a thing that he would want to handle it alone. We won't let him handle it all by himself. We just won't."

Suzanna did not respond. Arthur caught her eye as he passed in the front of the house, beeping his horn at the two of them, on his way out. When he was no longer in sight, Suzanna continued to look out in the distance, knowing it would only be a few minutes before Brant came to the house and that she would have to deliver a message from this stranger. Whether Brant knew the man or not, Suzanna knew it had to do with something he had been keeping from her - something from his past.

Dez sat quietly next to her mother on the porch swing as she observed a familiar look on her mother's face, the same expression she had the day she and Antonio visited her at the Cranbrook Institution in Yoakum, Texas. That day, when Dez went ahead of Antonio to be sure their mother was dressed and ready, Dez stood at the door and found Suzanna lost in thought. She was at her easel gazing out the window so deeply engrossed in thought that she did not respond when Dez called to her several times. Dez finally had to go over to her and very gently put her hand upon her shoulder so as not to frighten her. Today however, as Dez remembered that scene, she was determined to remain quiet and allow her mother to be alone with her thoughts.

As Suzanna anticipated Brant's arrival, she reflected on the memorable night of Arelius' and Adreanna's graduation when the two of them sat outside in the very swing she was now sitting in. After they talked and had such a wonderful evening being with the reunited family for supper at Dez's house, she recalled so vividly how her voice began to quiver a bit, and how Brant, so lovingly placed his finger gently on her lips. She recalled him saying to her, "*In time Suzanna, if you feel you want to talk about it, because you feel it will help you, please do. I'm here for you, and I hold nothing against you. I loved you then, I love you now even more Suzanna. There's not a thing on this earth that will make me feel differently, and you must know this. We are together now, and the past is our present. We are all together, and that's what matters. So, my dear, as this particular song has its title "Some-*

114

one to Watch over Me" I want you to know, I'm that someone who wants to, and I will watch over you." His very sweet question was,' Please, may I have this dance?"

Suzanna, even to the tiniest detail, remembered Brant extending his soft, Paul Sebastian scented, mono-grammed handkerchief to her, and after taking it, how she blotted her eyes and tucked it inside her blouse. She then stood up saying to him, "I want to dance with you forever."

Dez watched her mother as a smile appeared on her beautiful face. She could not know that this smile was a response to Suzanna's memories of her and Brant em-bracing each other tenderly and dancing slowly across the porch to the sound of, I Love You, Porgy and Don't Ever Leave Me. Suzanna remembered how secure and loved she felt in Brant's arms and with their first kiss since their encounter at Cranbrook. As the music stopped, she remembered thinking that their life together had just begun... again.

What brought her to her current situation was when she remembered the fact that Brant had stayed on the porch that night and told her to go ahead inside, that he would be in later. She knew he had things on his mind and so did not want to pry. She gave him the same re-spect that he had just earlier that night extended to her. Now with this new development staring her in the face, this newcomer, things were different. She had not asked him about his past. It had placed itself squarely in her lap.

This thought, and hearing Brant's voice, brought her back to the present.

"Here are my two most favorite people on this earth!" exclaimed Brant. "What a lovely picture the two of you are. Please allow me to take a photo so I can frame it for my study. I want to study it forever."

"What a good idea, Brant," said Suzanna. "We'll be right here when you get back with your camera."

"With all smiles," added Dez.

BEYOND ENCOUNTERS

CHAPTER FOURTEEN

Suzanna always knew *just* what to say to Brant at exactly the right moment ever since their reunion. Dez observed her mother as if trying to catch up on the lessons that were lost during all the years of separation. She had come to adore this woman, the mother she was so happy to have finally found.

After Brant was satisfied that he had captured the perfect shot, Suzanna told him that Dez and Eli were going to New Mexico in a few days.

"So, are you here to invite your aging parents to come along with the two of you, or would you prefer that your mother and I look in on the children?" he asked Dez.

"Well, now that *you've* mentioned it," her eyes speaking volumes, "Eli and I would like very much for you to look in on them. Eli's mother will be spending her vacation with them at the house, but it would be nice to know you're here as well."

"Oh," said Suzanna, "I'm so glad Alice will be here over the next couple of months! I really like her. We sure can talk when we are together."

"Well, it's all set," said Brant. "I guess I'll be getting a lot done over the next few months while Suzanna and Alice shop and frequent the new Soup & Subs on the square in town."

"Brant," implored Suzanna, "you know you can do those things with us. I love you so. Oh my, I almost forgot." She stood up to retrieve the card from the kitchen.

Puzzled, Brant looked at her when she returned as she handed him the card.

"Brant, dear, there was a man who came here today looking for you. His name was Evan Kinkaid. He's still here in Hallettsville and will be leaving tomorrow evening." She spoke with an obvious edge in her voice. "He said his father knew your mother, Candace, and he promised his father before he died that he would see to it you received something his father wanted you to have."

Brant was standing now, holding the card at waist level with his gaze frozen on his wife. The more she revealed, the faster his heart raced.

Suzanna continued. "He brought it to give to you and

said he planned to go to New York to care for some of his father's other interests. He wanted to meet with you so he could return to New York tomorrow."

Brant still stood frozen. He and Suzanna locked gazes as she continued.

"He was a pleasant man, I must say - very respectful. He appeared to be a bit older than you. He said he was staying at the Travel Lodge just outside of town and hoped very much that you would meet with him before he left. He seemed determined to carry out his father's wishes."

Brant spoke almost inaudibly. "That's interesting, because for some time now I've been thinking about my life in Paris."

"You mean your life after I left, dear?"

He sat back down in his chair. He seemed to be calming down a bit. Holding the card with both hands, he stared down at it as he continued.

"No, not quite. Actually, it was before we even met. It was when I was a little boy. A memory comes to my mind that takes me back to the living room of our house in Paris. I see my mother and this man in the living room. I thought I was well hidden behind the sofa when I heard the man say loudly, 'A boy should know! A boy should know!' The next day the man came back. When my mother went to the kitchen to get him something to drink, he made it known that he saw me hiding the day before. He said he saw my hat and that if I didn't want to be found out while I was hiding, I should be as still as a frozen snake. It gave me chills. I remember shaking a bit after he said that. Then I focused on the fact that he said a "frozen snake". Even still, I ran to my room and closed the door and locked it."

Dez was on the edge of her seat. "Oh my, Dad, how frightening it all sounds! Who was that man?"

"Dez, I have wondered that all these years, especially when those memories would flood into my mind."

"Were those the thoughts you wanted to think on after the children's graduation, Brant, when you told me you wanted to stay outside for a bit longer?"

"Yes, Suzanna, they did come to mind. I just wanted to make some sense of them. Well, I didn't."

"The man who came looking for you may be able to shed light on those thoughts, Brant," Suzanna said as she moved near to him and put her hand on his shoulder.

Shaking his head, Brant said, "I certainly have no idea who this man is nor what it is that he wants to give me."

"Dad, would you like Eli to go with you to see him tomorrow? We're not leaving for another few days."

"You know, Dez, I would like that very much. I'd like us to stick close together - as close as possible now."

Suzanna looked at Dez, smiled, and said, "You can be sure we feel the same way you do, dear."

Dez confirmed those feelings by giving Brant a hug, after which she reached over and hugged Suzanna saying, "I'll tell Eli what's happening and you can call him tonight to let him know when you'd like to go see Mr. Evan Kinkaid."

"Thank you, Dez. I love you and Eli. And this lady

right here," turning to Suzanna with a warm smile, "I love her so much."

"I love you very much too, Brant," said Suzanna.

Brant called Eli when he thought he had given Dez enough time to get home and tell him the details he had shared with her about Evan Kinkaid.

Eli reassured Brant over the phone, "Dez told me about what's going on. I'm so glad you want me to accompany you tomorrow. Just tell me when you'd like to go, I'll be there and I'll drive you to meet with Mr. Kinkaid."

Brant let a sigh of relief escape his lips. "Eli, I knew I could count on you! Let's do this thing early in the morning. It seems he has an agenda and has to get going and I certainly don't want to be the one holding him up. Seems he has a lot to do for his father. How about 7:30 in the morning and we'll stop for coffee at the Internet Café?"

"That'll be just fine, Brant. I'll see you then, have a nice night."

"Thank you, Eli. Oh, and by the way, I do appreciate Arelius helping when Arthur gets the feed from your store. He comes out with Arthur and they have it all unloaded in such a short period of time. That boy is really going to make some young lady a good husband."

"I agree on all counts, Brant. He certainly helps out at the store. I think he likes the business."

"You do have a good business. Keep up the good work."

"My! Thank you, Brant. Dez and I will never forget

the help you gave us to rebuild the feed store after that storm. You can count on me to give it my best shot in keeping up the *good work* as you put it."

"It was the least I could do for the two of you. I'm just so happy you allowed me to help. Well, I'll let you go now, Eli, goodnight."

"Goodnight, Brant. I'll see you in the morning."

BEYOND ENCOUNTERS

CHAPTER FIFTEEN

As Eli's and Brant's conversation went on, Dez reflected on the first time they ever saw Brant as the newcomer at the Internet Café. "How things have changed," she said in a low voice.

"Sounds like you and Dad get along really well," Dez said as he finally hung up the phone.

"I think so. I've come to like him, although we didn't hit it off at first. What a story! I agree with Bob Lacy - someone should write about it."

"This evening Adreanna said I should gather all my poems and have them published."

"She has a good point there, Dez. You might want to give that some serious thought."

"I just may do that. But the serious thought I have

on my mind at the moment is soaking in my favorite bubble bath, then curling up with you and doing some serious sleeping."

"Oh. I thought I was going to hear something else, "said Eli, feigning a frown.

"And what might that have been?"

"After all this time, do you really have to ask what's on my mind when you begin your sentence the way you did?"

"Yes, I'm afraid I still must ask. As you can tell, my mind is elsewhere. There are just so many things to think about: your mom, Jake, and now what you, Adreanna, and Mr. Lacy have said about me writing... all of that *and* the fact that I'm really tired, well, my mind certainly wasn't where yours was."

Eli smiled, the dimple in his left cheek clearly visible, and softly said, "May I run your bath, li'l Red Riding Hood?"

"How thoughtful of you, honey, that would be very nice. I have things I would like to think over as I soak. Thank you, you are so sweet." She leaned in to kiss his forehead, anticipating that, as she did, he would reach to kiss her as well. He did. Very softly he kissed the very small red birthmark in the soft sink of her neck.

"I know you did that for my benefit," he whispered. "Thank you. You are truly sweet. I enjoyed it."

"You are one *easy to please* man, I must say, and I love you."

"I love you too, Dez. Now let me run your bath before you forget you're tired."

Sliding into the warmth of the bubbly bathwater, she placed her head on the wide rim of the old claw-foot tub, took a deep breath, let it out unhurriedly and then closed her eyes. After only a few seconds she ever-so-slowly opened them again and looked up at the ceiling as if searching for the focal point that would enable her to do serious meditation. She recalled that she and Eli had learned the 'focal point theory' during two separate Lamaze classes they took in preparation for the birth of Arelius and Adreanna.

Dez committed to memory the lessons from her instructor, Cheryl Henke, as if she had just left the classroom at the medical center and certainly not where she found herself some seventeen years previous. During one of the classes, Dez fondly remembered when Cheryl smiled and told her as Eli held the pillow underneath her head, "Now, Dez, you can't seem to locate a focal point. I can tell."

Dez remembered the beautiful smile Cheryl had and never once saw her frown in all the classes she and Eli attended under her instruction.

"Let's find one for you," Cheryl said, referring to the focal point. "There, do you see that small opening next to the vent on the ceiling there?" Cheryl asked as she pointed to the middle of the ceiling.

"Yes, I looked all over that spot. I think that's a

good focal point, thank you," said Dez. "I hope there'll be something like this one in the hospital when it's time."

Cheryl nodded, "There's always a focal point to be found, and I know your coach will help you when the time comes, won't you, Eli?"

"For sure," Eli spoke up.

Cheryl continued, "The two of you are doing so well. When I go in to deliver this one *I'm* carrying, I hope I'll do as well as I know *you* will, Dez." But there was a hint of doubt in her voice.

"I have no doubt you'll remember everything you're instructing us, Cheryl," Dez assured her. "Bob will be the best coach for you."

Eli became very good friends with Cheryl's husband, Bob, during the classes. At the reunion of the Lamaze classmates, with their new arrivals, all of the men were not only exchanging their experiences from the labor room, but were also changing diapers throughout the reunion.

This reflection back to that time calmed her, but it was the soaking bath that was the most relaxing. Dez allowed herself to think upon the past months. She did indeed find something to focus on as she gazed up. The knots in the grain of the wood ceiling produced what appeared to be the face of a panda bear. Her mind again wandered, this time back to two incidences, one after the other: The occasion when Eli had gone to Seattle to be with his mother after the doctor explained what multiple myeloma was, and also to the time she traveled to Eagle Pass to be with Jake during his hospitalization. Jake's neighbor, Dorothy, called to say she had taken him to the hospital because of the painful sickle cell crisis he was experiencing.

Dez remembered that day when she arrived at the hospital. Jake was asleep. After checking in on him and leaving him a basket of candies and a stuffed animal, her custom was to find the nurse who had been assigned to him, in order to go over his lab reports. All it took was that first time for the nurses to know this would be the custom for any future visits that Dez would make to be with her son. With such regular visits to the hospital, the nurses got into the habit of having Jake's chart nearby, as they knew for a certainty that Dez would be returning to the desk for a report on her son as soon as she checked in on him.

Now, with only three days before their vacation, three days before they were scheduled to go to New Mexico with hopes of it being a snowed-in rendezvous, Evan Kinkaid had come onto the scene - as if everything Eli and Dez were going through for the last few months before this vacation wasn't enough. There was certainly a lot going on in their lives.

Meanwhile, back on the Chamberlain's front-porch, Brant and Suzanna enjoyed the night air as they watched for the last light to go out in the Ortello house.

Suzanna held Brant's hand gently. "Brant, this could be the end of what has plagued you since childhood, something that was already hard-pressing long before what went on in our lives. Now, hopefully it can truly be a thing of the past after you meet with Mr. Kinkaid tomorrow."

He nodded in agreement. "I know you're right Suzanna LeAnn, but we'll have to wait to see if that will be the case. Until then, let's use the rest of the evening to watch the lights go out at the children's house. I get such satisfaction from doing that."

She curled up under his protective arm. "I have the same feeling Brant, it gives me the sense that we're watching over them. I won't let anything get in the way of our doing this, now that we are all together."

Brant gave Suzanna a warm embrace. He knew she meant every word and agreed with her wholeheartedly. They cuddled on the porch swing and remained quiet as they took in the night's sounds.

As Dez continued to soak in the old fashioned tub, thinking of her trip to Eagle Pass while Eli was in Seattle with his mother, Eli was thinking about the scheduled meeting his mother's doctor had set up with the family in regard to her newly diagnosed disease, multiple myeloma.

The oncologist, Dr. Daniel Goldman, from a medical center located on a military base in San Antonio, Texas, had formally written Eli to set up a time they could get together to discuss what was in store for his mother. He was very informative in his letter.

A chill went through Eli as he thought about what had been revealed during that initial conference with the doctor in Seattle, Washington, as well as the information Dr. Goldman had included in his letter. He remembered in bold print the word "**Oncology**" and the information about the medical center. It was described as a nationally recognized, worldwide military referral center, providing expedient, state of the art, comprehensive and multidisciplinary cancer therapy.

He remembered being somewhat satisfied by the fact that there were specialists available in many areas such as medical oncology, malignant and nonmalignant hematology, and that there was an outpatient chemotherapy clinic and an emergency walk-in clinic.

Also comforting was the fact that the Oncology Nurse Specialist would provide education and counseling for his mother that would include comprehensive information on the diagnosis and a proposed treatment plan. He recognized the fact that his mother and the family needed to be taught how to manage treatment related side effects. He was told that the oncology clinical nurse specialist would be available to the staff assisting Alice with her chemotherapy.

Many of the terms Dr. Goldman used in his letter were familiar to Eli. Also included in the letter were directions for Eli and his family; he had memorized every detail.

Eli shivered as he pulled the light quilt to his chin while stretched out in the recliner. He shook his head as if to get the unpleasant thoughts far removed from him, but the whole visit was on his mind as it replayed itself slowly as he lay there.

Alice had gone to Texas early this time in order to keep the consultation with the oncologist that her doctor in Seattle had scheduled. Eli, his wife, and his siblings sat quietly in the doctor's office with Alice, all eager to know what they did not know.

Dr. Goldman, a tall, young, imposing man, with slightly graying temples, and wire glasses framing gentle brown eyes, entered the room holding a clip-board under his arm. Facing the family, he leaned back against the mahogany desk. His smile was reassuring. "I'm so glad we could get together to talk about the things that have happened and that are currently going on with your mother. It's very important that Alice have the support of the family at this time, and I have no doubt that she does. In the months ahead, she will experience side effects from the prednisone medication that her doctor has already put her on. Alice," he directed his attention to her, "Are you experiencing any of the side effects your doctor discussed with you?"

Nodding, she said, "I'm alright."

One of Eli's sisters, Debbie, spoke up and said, "Mom isn't a complainer, perhaps we should know what side effects you're referring to, Doctor."

"Side effects of treatment with prednisone can be depression, euphoria, hypertension, nausea, anorexia, high blood sugar levels, and increased susceptibility to infection. Even still," he addressed Alice, "the important thing is for you to take the medication. And if you do experience some of these things, we will try to find the best medication to offset them and make the side effects manageable."

Eli shivered at the memory, then rose from the recliner, placed the quilt across the back and made his way to bed. Both he and Dez were simultaneously recalling the activity of recent months. As they each realized how exhausted they were, a thought occurred to them about postponing the New Mexico trip. But before Eli reached the bed, he determined that they would indeed keep their vacation plans.

As Dez sat at her vanity brushing her hair, Eli said, "You know, Dez, the thought of postponing our trip passed through my mind…but I was thinking just now, we should keep our plans. In fact, it's settled, we will keep them."

"I thought about the same thing, but my thought was to cancel the trip."

"I feel we should go, unless circumstances dictate otherwise."

"Well, I won't balk at that. Let's just hope all goes well for our trip."

When they met each other in bed after they both had opportunity to meditate on their thoughts, Eli reiterated to Dez, "I'm really glad Brant wants me to go with him in the morning to meet this Kinkaid guy. I wonder what it's about. It must be pretty important for him to come here to personally deliver what his father gave him to give your dad."

"Well, by tomorrow afternoon we should know why he has come here. I'm hoping there won't be a problem, things are going so well now, with all of us together I mean," she said as she fluffed her pillow.

"Yes, I know. We have a lot of things behind us true, Dez, but there are things we have yet to face. Are you ready?"

"I'm ready, Eli, we can face them together and that will make things okay. Try not to worry too much about Alice and Jake. I know they're on your mind. They're on my mind too. I'm glad we've decided to go on the trip and I hope we get tons of snow while there. I won't care a bit if we get snowed in the whole time we're there."

"Now you're talking. Don't we leave tomorrow?" asked Eli.

"No," she chuckled, "in a few days, but I feel refreshed now after that fantastic soak. You do know me, don't you? Thank you, honey."

"After the years of being with you, I've taken note of you in so many ways. It'll be morning and time to go with your father if I start listing them now."

"How sweet," Dez responded.

With all said, the last of the lights went off in their house.

BEYOND ENCOUNTERS

CHAPTER SIXTEEN

Six months prior to the planned trip to Ruidoso, things were not as good for Eli and Dez as they were now.

Eli's mother, Alice, had been trying with each trip to Hallettsville to inform Eli about the tests that had been done on her and the fact that she had not gone back for the results. Instead, when she left Seattle, Washington for these extended stays, she had become close to Suzanna, even more so than with the friends she had come to know over the years in Hallettsville.

Many times Alice reflected on how her friends had taken her to Eli and Dez's that memorable day on their way to San Antonio to see the Hemisphere Tower. The group of them stopped by her son's house and waited for Alice to run in and leave a surprise note about her popping in to Hallettsville to get with her friends for a few days. It was that embarrassing time when Alice heard a noise while she was getting the beautiful glass pitcher from the refrigerator to have a glass of water, only to come to the realization that she was not as alone in the house as she thought. She met Eli and Dez, face to face, as they were coming down the stairs to see what the noise in the kitchen was about. After that particular encounter there were no more surprise visits.

When Alice returned home to Seattle after the unforgettable double graduation of her grandchildren, Arelius and Adreanna, she knew she had to face the results of the medical tests. She informed her doctor that she preferred not to know until after her two grandchildren graduated, and that when she returned home she would come to see him. When she made that visit to the doctor's office, it was a visit that she would keep to herself and away from her son. She was not ready to inform him of the diagnosis.

Alice was diagnosed with multiple myeloma, an incurable, but treatable disease. It was a disease that she had never heard of and could hardly pronounce at first, but as time went on, not only did it become easy to say, but she heard it spoken more and more often as she moved through her day-to-day activities. When she watched a program on television, the term would be heard. When she read Reader's Digest, something that she had done for years, without even noticing those words, she now saw them as if the articles on the condition were printed specifically for her.

The doctor comforted her. "This diagnosis is no doubt overwhelming you, Alice, but it is important to remember that there are several promising new therapies that are helping patients live longer, healthier lives."

"Wait," Alice said to her doctor, "Are you telling me I have cancer, and that I'm going to die?"

"Alice, multiple myeloma is a rare form of cancer."

"Wait," Alice interrupted again and said, "I'm ready to talk with my son. I'll get back with you about it."

On every visit that Alice made to Texas, Suzanna found some way to bring up Alice's marital status and why she had never sought to change it. Alice's predictable response always included long, loving descriptions of her late husband and how she just could never find anyone to fill his shoes. Suzanna would try to reason with her from a psychological standpoint, but typically was out-reasoned by her long-time friend.

On one such visit, while they enjoyed lunch together at the Internet Café, Alice took Suzanna into her confidence. During the inevitable encouragement to find a life-mate, Alice told her the news. She had kept it from Eli and Dezeray as long as she could, but now, with recurring episodes of pain, Alice felt it was time to talk with her son and hoped he would understand her refraining from informing him earlier. Suzanna was supportive, as always, and assured her that Eli was a reasonable man and would understand.

On her next visit and after informing Eli and the family of her condition, she found that Suzanna was right – Eli understood and was very supportive, so much so that on the plane home, she and Eli were *both* on their way to Seattle. Dez called Alice's doctor to inform him that Alice would be in his office Monday morning, and that Eli, her son, would be accompanying her.

They left on Friday afternoon, and the first thing Monday morning Eli and Alice were sitting in the waiting room in anxious anticipation of being called into the doctor's office.

"Alice Ortello," the nurse called out. "The doctor will see you now."

Eli and Alice each took a deep breath, got up and went into the office. After introducing Eli, Alice asked the doctor to explain to her son exactly what she was suffering from. She and Eli took their seats in the chairs in front of the doctor's dark, paper-cluttered desk.

He spoke very calmly. "Eli, your mother has a medical condition called multiple myeloma."

"Please, Doctor," Eli pleaded, "Explain so that we will know what we're dealing with here."

"Of course, Eli," said the doctor, moving to sit against the front of his desk. "Multiple myeloma is a rare form of cancer characterized by excessive production and improper function of certain plasma cells found in the bone marrow. Plasma cells are a type of white blood cell and are produced in the bone marrow and eventually enter the bloodstream. Excessive plasma cells may eventually mass together to form a tumor, or tumors, in various sites of the body, especially the bone marrow. If only a single tumor is present, the term 'solitary plasmacytoma' is used. When multiple tumors are present, as is the case with your mother, the term 'multiple myeloma' is used.

Eli gently cradled his mother's hand in his.

The doctor continued. "Plasma cells are a key component of the immune system and they secrete a substance known as myeloma proteins or 'M-proteins', a type of antibody. Antibodies are special proteins that the body produces to combat invading microorganisms, toxins, or other foreign substances. Overproduction of plasma cells in affected individuals results in abnormally high levels of these proteins within the body."

The doctor noticed Eli was listening intently. Continuing, he said, "I know all of this medical talk can go over your head, but I feel you understand what is happening with your mother, Eli, am I right?"

"I do have an idea, now that you have laid it out,

Doctor. My next question has to be asked, and I know Mom should be aware of the answer to it."

"Prognosis?" anticipated the doctor.

"Yes," Eli nodded his head, patting Alice's hand.

The doctor paused, took a deep breath and sat down in a third chair next to Alice. "It's imperative that we perform exams and administer tests to learn the extent of the cancer within her body, especially whether the disease has spread from the original site to other parts. It is also important to know the stage of the disease in order to, not only answer that question, but plan the best treatment for Alice."

He sat back and crossed his legs. Looking at Eli he continued.

"*Staging* is a careful attempt to find out what parts of the body are affected by the cancer. Treatment decisions depend on these findings. Results of Alice's exam, blood tests, and bone marrow tests can help us determine the stage of the disease. In addition, staging will, in her case, involve a series of x-rays to determine the number and size of tumors in the bones."

He next turned to Alice. "Alice, have you been experiencing pain in your back, perhaps your ribs as well?"

"Yes, I have," she said, nodding her head.

"Physically, that is the most known major symptom of multiple myeloma; bone pain, especially in the back and the ribs. As far as blood tests are concerned, low levels of circulating red blood cells, or anemia, are detected, resulting in weakness, fatigue, and lack of color and kidney abnormalities. In most cases, affected individuals are more susceptible to bacterial infections, such as pneumonia."

"Doctor," Eli interrupted. "Just what causes multiple myeloma?"

"Eli, the exact cause of multiple myeloma is unknown. There are approximately forty-five thousand people in the United States living with multiple myeloma and an estimated fifteen thousand new cases of multiple myeloma are diagnosed each year. And now, as for an answer to your question about the prognosis, once a bone marrow disease has been diagnosed, it has a prognosis of about five years. Survival of multiple myeloma patients could vary from months to years, depending on the extent of the cancer, overall condition of the patient, as well as their response to treatments and the duration of their response."

Rising, he walked around his desk and sat down in his large leather chair. Alice held Eli's hand with both of hers.

The doctor went on to say, "Multiple myeloma may be found as part of a routine physical exam before patients have symptoms of the disease. When patients do have symptoms, the doctor asks about their personal and family medical history and does a complete physical exam. In addition to checking general signs of health, the doctor may order a number of tests to determine the cause of the symptoms. If a patient has bone pain, *x-rays* can show whether any bones are damaged or broken. Samples of the patient's blood and urine are checked to see whether they contain high levels of antibody proteins I mentioned before, called *M proteins*. The doctor also may do a *bone marrow aspiration* and/or a *bone marrow biopsy* to check for myeloma cells. In an aspiration, the doctor inserts a needle into the hip bone or breast bone to withdraw a sample of fluid and cells from the bone marrow. To do a biopsy, the doctor uses a larger needle to remove a sample of solid tissue from the marrow. A *pathologist* examines the samples under a microscope to see whether myeloma cells are present."

"Well, Doctor," Eli took a deep breath, "All of this is a bit much for us at the moment. May we please have printed information to help us explain these things to the family?"

"Of course, Eli." He crossed the room to extract a pamphlet from a cabinet, and handing it to Eli he explained, "Also, at times I arrange meetings between patients, their families and the doctors with whom I collaborate with about any particular disease that has affected the families' loved ones. These doctors can be located in different places around the country. I actually consult with one less than two hours from where you live Eli, in San Antonio. He is a bit young, but his credentials speak for themselves in an outstanding way. He is an oncology doctor at a medical center on one of the military bases there. Your mother will be able to use those medical services."

"Doctor," Eli said rising as he accepted the pamphlets, "we would appreciate that very much. That would be very good if you could arrange such a meeting for us, because I will probably forget everything you have told me as soon as we leave this office. I know my family will be happy about anything you can arrange. Thank you very much."

"Yes" Alice agreed, "I would appreciate that too."
She stood to shake his hand.

"Now, Alice," the doctor patted the top of her hand, "I will work very closely with you to make everything understandable along the way as we help you with your illness."

"I feel confident that what you say is true, Doctor, but now my son must get home to his family. I know they are worried about him as well. Thank you again, Doctor."

"You are very welcome, Alice. I will be seeing you soon. My nurse will call you to set up your next appointment."

Alice and Eli left the doctor's office arm in arm. Before getting into Alice's car to drive her home, Eli gave her a long hug and said, "Mom, everything will be alright. Dez and I, as well as the children, are with you all the way on this. I love you very much. I won't tell you not to worry; I'll just ask you to try not to be overly worried about this. We'll get informed about it so we'll know how to better handle it. Just knowing dispels a lot of fears."

"You've already made me feel better, son. Now, how about a nice big slice of my pecan pie I just made."

"That sounds great… got milk?" Eli asked with a smile.

BEYOND ENCOUNTERS

CHAPTER SEVENTEEN

Six months before their Ruidoso getaway, the Ortello couple reeled from the shock of Eli's mother's illness. While Eli was in Seattle with Alice, Dorothy, Jake's friend from Eagle Pass, called Dez to inform her that she had taken Jake to the hospital due to a sickle cell crisis, and because he was in such pain, it was unbearable for him to stay at his apartment.

Dez made preparations to travel to Eagle Pass to be with him. She tied up loose ends and reviewed with Arelius Eli's instructions for managing the feed store while both of his parents were away from home.

Adreanna sensed that her mother may be tense from the news about Jake, and so brought her mother a cool glass of water. She gave Dez a long hug and said, "He'll be alright until you get there. I know you're going. You're always there for him. I love you, Mother. He's so used to going into the hospital now. He'll tell them just what to do and he'll be fine."

Dez patted her daughter on the back. "I know he will be okay," said Dez, "He sure has turned out to be a self-sufficient young man."

"Yes," said Adreanna, "He's been that for a long time now."

Dez pulled away and gazed lovingly into Adreanna's eyes. "I agree." She gently laid her hand on Adreanna's cheek. "Now are you and Arelius going to be alright while your dad and I are away?"

"Yes, Mother, we've left behind most of our sibling rivalry and laugh about it now. Arelius will have his hands full with the feed store, and I'll take care of visiting Grandmother Suzanna and Grandfather Brant. Mother, how is Grandma Alice? Has Dad called about how she is?"

"Not yet. Try not to worry Adreanna, Daddy will talk with all of us when he gets back, and just as soon as Jake gets out of the hospital, I'll be back too."

When Dez arrived at the hospital, Rachel was in Jake's hospital room sitting in a chair beside his bed. She ran to Dez as she came in. It was the first time Rachel had seen Jake go through severe episodes of pain and it was almost unbearable for her to see him hurt so badly. Dez had a pretty good idea why Rachel ran to her for an embrace and Rachel's tears erased any doubt.

"I had no idea, Mrs. Ortello that Jake went through this with his sickle cell crises. When Penny and I saw him at the hospital in Hallettsville, he wasn't in as much pain as I see him in now. I'm so glad he is asleep at the moment."

"I'm so glad you're here, Rachel. I know Jake is too. Penny was a very important part of Jake's life, and he misses her very much."

The both of them were in tears as Dez was feeling the loss of Penny. Dez continued, "Since she isn't here to be with him I have no doubt that he's really happy that she introduced you to him."

"I miss Penny so much too. She and I visited Jake so many times that I knew just how to get here."

She wiped the tears from her cheeks as Dez set her packages on the corner chair.

"You've come a long way, Rachel. It shows you care a lot about Jake."

"Yes, I do. He said he was going to tell you that he gave me his senior ring."

"Yes, I called him to let him know about our trip to New Mexico, and he mentioned it. In fact, at that time he told me that the two of you get along really well, and that you are a very mature young lady."

The tears were beginning to go away from both their eyes as they began to talk about the relationship, at which point Jake stirred with a bit of a moan as he went back to sleep. They smiled at each other as Dez said, "I guess he's trying to be part of our conversation about the two of you. Rachel, I'll be right back, I want to check with his nurse about his lab results. Are you okay?"

"Yes, I'm okay now, thank you. I'm so glad you made it."

Dez hugged her again and left for the nurse's station. Jake's nurse had his chart ready to let Dez know the usual things she was concerned about, namely, his hemoglobin red count, white count, temp, blood pressure - the things that would give Dez insight as to how Jake was fairing with this particular sickle cell crisis.

After being satisfied that things were being handled in the best way for Jake, Dez commended the nurses on their care of her son. Once Jake's condition stabilized, he was normally back at home within a few days, and Dez too, would be home in Hallettsville.

As Eli and Dez lay in bed after each had recalled the events about Alice and Jake, they talked about their planned trip to Ruidoso. They had a lot to talk about, especially about why this Evan Kinkaid had come to Hallettsville all the way from Paris, France, other than that he just wanted to give Brant something he had promised his father he would give him.

"Well," began Dez, "Mother said Mr. Kinkaid's father knew Daddy's mother, Candace. I wonder just how well he knew her and if it has something to do with *her*."

"It could be a number of things, Dez; I just think we should wait 'til tomorrow, and, well, for the moment, pretend we're already snowed-in at our condo in Ruidoso."

"You know, Eli, I'm sure you're right. Let's do just that. I'm going to pretend I'm there sleeping, it's caught up to me again."

Dez kissed Eli with a very quick peck on his fading dimple which disappeared after she mentioned the idea about sleeping. Eli dismissed his idea and curled up next to her. Not a minute passed before they both fell into a deep sleep.

All of a sudden there was a very loud pounding on the patio door upstairs on the balcony. As usual Dez was sleeping soundly and heard nothing. Eli, however, was a light sleeper and immediately sat up and looked in the direction of the patio door. In the yellow lighting he clearly discerned a man. Eli's thoughts raced. How in the world did he get up to the balcony in the first place? It's late and why is he there? I've never seen this man before, who is he?

The thought did run through Eli's mind that this might be Evan Kinkaid, the one he and Dez were just talking about. Eli thought to himself, *'Am I dreaming? I must be dreaming, this can't be happening. Just look at Dez - she didn't hear anything, she is sound asleep. Anyone would have heard that loud of a knock. I must be dreaming.*

So Eli laid his head back down on his pillow and tightly squeezed his eyes together in an effort to get the picture of the man out of his mind. It was not another minute before he heard another loud knock. Eli rose up again, but this time he got up out of the bed and went to the patio door.

There, outside his door, he saw a man wearing a stylish black beret. He had a box. Eli saw the man's lips moving as if saying, '*Open the door, I need to speak with you.*' Eli asked, "Why are you here, what do you want?"

The man said in a louder voice, "Open the door, I have to give you this box."

Eli said, "You're Evan Kinkaid. You're supposed to give that to Brant. I'm not Brant!"

The man said, "Yes, I know you're not Brant. But you must take this box now, tonight."

"No!" Eli said emphatically, "Just wait until morning and you give it to him!"

The man said, "If you don't take this box tonight, you'll be sorry. Take it!"

"No!" said Eli, "I don't want that box! I don't want it I tell you! I don't want that box! I don't want that box!"

Eli repeated the phrase, 'I don't want that box!' over and over and over, waking to Dez shaking his shoulders. "Eli! Wake up! Wake up, Eli! Honey, you're dreaming! There is *no* one; there *is* no box, Eli!"

Eli awoke breathless and looked over at the patio door. There was no one there... only darkness. After gathering his wits, he sighed and flopped back down on the pillow. Disconcerted, he said, "I can't wait 'til morning to get this mystery business over with concerning Evan Kinkaid and Brant!"

BEYOND ENCOUNTERS

CHAPTER EIGHTEEN

Morning could not have come sooner for Eli, or for Brant, who also had been up several times during the night as if to hurry morning's arrival. He was anxious to meet Evan Kinkaid, and even more anxious to know what the real reason was for his arrival to the States.

During the sleepless night, Brant took time to ponder his thoughts. His memory took him back to growing up with his new family after his mother married Mr. Haggerty. That marriage came with an instantly larger family. It included Arthur and Lance. He could not help but wonder about his early childhood and just what Mr. Kinkaid was in Hallettsville for.

He thought of the time not too long after his mother and Mr. Haggerty were married that his new step-brothers showed him just how much they liked him. Once when Brant had ventured farther from the house than he normally would, a bully from the neighborhood, with his two lanky looking sidekicks, approached Brant. They obviously saw him as an easy one to use for a little fun. The bullies seemed intent on leaving Brant lying in the mud puddle not too far from where he stood.

As soon as it became obvious that this was escalating into an incident, Lance left their front porch and ran inside the house to let Arthur know about it. The both of them made haste to the scene just in time for Arthur to pull Brant away from the intended push coming from the bully...and classically, the bully himself fell into the mud puddle with a splat. It was feat by Arthur that Brant never forgot. At that point Brant looked up to Arthur as the big brother and protector, and Lance as the loyal one who would help in the best way that he could, being the youngest of the three. Brant knew that Lance was the real reason he was spared from the clutches of the bully because Arthur made it known that his little brother deserved the credit. At that, Brant hugged Lance and said, "Thank you, Lance, I know I can count on you whenever trouble finds me."

Arthur, the oldest of the brothers, proved to be very responsible from early on when he was put in position to look after Lance, when at times it only meant to watch him when his mother was cooking, or washing, or doing things that merited her attention away from Baby

Lance, Toddler Lance, the Terrible-twos Lance, and so on. Lance obviously found it quite amusing when he understood that "with every action there is an equal and opposite reaction" at about the age of fifteen months. Like others at his young age, he would hurl his favorite toy out of his crib, cry like he had broken an arm, and then he would wait. When Arthur did not retrieve it fast enough his tears fell faster and his screams louder, but once the toy was in his hand, he immediately fell silent and content - until Arthur walked into the next room and then the scene began again.

Lance's attitude changed almost immediately when Brant came into the family. He was distracted from annoying Arthur, with the challenge of how to get this new guy to do his chores, or to help with his homework. Brant was accommodating in both areas to the happiness of Lance. Whether it was the fact that Brant was so helpful to him as "the little brother he never had" or the fact that Brant spared him a lot of discipline, it was of no account to Lance.

He was about as care free as he could be at all ages. He was content if no one other than his beloved brothers entered his world and he rarely, if ever, allowed anyone else to get close to him, an early indication of the kind of person Lance would grow up to be. True to the early expectations of his brothers, Lance was as carefree now as he was back then.

Brant, however, was one that looked at the person

next to him as someone to get to know, even that bully who fell to the mud. His list of friends surpassed both Arthur's and Lance's put together. He had a magnetizing force about himself. Perhaps that's what drew the bully and his lanky looking pals to him. He could reason the socks off the miser who owned only one pair. He became an asset in his father's shoe business in Brighton, England, and no doubt was responsible for it reaching its year to year peak in sales.

Brant's thoughts brought him back to reality as the sun began to peek over the horizon, lighting up the room and then rousing the birds in the trees just outside his bedroom window. He was glad the morning was finally here on this most promising day.

Evan Kinkaid desired morning to hurry its arrival. He had also spent a restless night. His memories had taken him back to the day that his father lay sleeping in a hospital bed by the window in the very old Batronce` DuGaul Hospital in Paris. Evan had specifically requested this particular room because of its view of Yatonse Gardens. He could hear his father talking to him about things he had never heard before.

His thoughts were startled to the present day when

the telephone rang. He sat up quickly, picking up the receiver in the same motion of his raising up from the bed. "Hello," Evan said with enthusiasm in his voice.

"Hello, my name is Brant Chamberlain. My wife gave me this number to reach a Mr. Evan Kinkaid."

"Yes, Mr. Chamberlain, I'm Evan Kinkaid. Thank you very much for calling. My father made me promise to hand deliver a letter to you, and a package. He knew your mother in Paris. May we meet so I can do this? I will not feel satisfied until it is done."

"I am just as eager to know what this is about as you are to fulfill the obligation. May we meet in a public place?"

Evan sensed Brant's apprehension.

"Most assuredly," Evan readily replied. "Where would you like to meet?"

"There is a restaurant near the Travel Lodge where you're staying called, *Texas Sized Everything*. Perhaps you saw it?" asked Brant.

"Yes, yes, I did. What time would you like to meet there?' asked Evan.

"Would nine o'clock be okay with you?"

"Yes, Mr. Chamberlain that would be good."

Brant asked, "How will we know each other?"

"I'll keep my French cap on, but I think you will recognize me without a hat."

"Okay," said Brant. After hanging up, Brant wondered what he meant. *Could it be that I know him? Have*

I seen him before? Now I'm really curious.

Eli was in front of Brant's house at 7:30 sharp, as agreed. After breakfast at the Internet Café, they went to the restaurant to meet Mr. Kinkaid.

Upon arrival at the restaurant Brant looked very slowly around. He picked out a person who for some reason seemed to fit the name Evan. However, this particular man did not have a hat on… yet Brant went over to the table.

"You're Evan Kinkaid."

The man rose and extended his hand. "I did tell you that you would recognize me without my hat being on, and I myself had a feeling that you were Brant Chamberlain the second you walked through the door."

As the two of them talked, Eli formed his own thoughts as to why the two of them recognized each other. He remained quiet and waited to be introduced.

It was as if Brant heard Eli's thoughts.

"I'm sorry," Brant said, "Mr. Kinkaid, this is my son-in-law, Eli. Eli, this is Mr. Kinkaid."

"It's nice to meet you, Eli."

They shook hands.

"Yes, same here," Eli nodded his head.

Evan Kinkaid's chauffeur remained in the car while his employer carried out his business. The chauffeur had been with Evan's father before Evan was born and now faithfully served him. He was a very dependable man, looking after Evan as if his job required he serve also as his body guard.

"Shall we take care of this matter here, Mr. Chamberlain?" asked Evan.

"Yes, that would be fine."

BEYOND ENCOUNTERS

CHAPTER NINTEEN

As Brant and Mr. Kinkaid settled at a table, Eli, respecting their privacy, politely excused himself and sat at a nearby booth, close enough to watch his father-in-law, but not too close that he could eavesdrop. He sipped his coffee, intently watching Brant's face.

As the two men spoke, Eli slipped into a series of memories about his mother, when things were not going so well for her. It was such a horrible revelation about the multiple myeloma. It began to take its toll on Alice. With each visit to Seattle, he noticed a marked change in her physical appearance, and he was helpless to do anything about it. Eventually, the sunrise she witnessed and so enjoyed each morning in the back room of her son's house in Hallettsville became the sunset of her life as she succumbed to the disease on October 14, 1993.

These thoughts Eli had as he sat there watching Brant and Mr. Kinkaid, remembering that Mr. Kinkaid had only recently lost his father. With such a thought, he was compelled to continue to think upon his own losses.

It seemed to be a time of so many losses of loved ones. On February 15, 1996, Dez's Aunt Ethel, was not feeling well and thought she had better go to the emergency room. They wanted to keep her at the County Medical Center overnight only for observation. Her children were called back to the hospital and informed that she died.

He then thought about when Dez was called to the hospital in regard to one of Uncle Arthur's children. Come to find out, upon arriving at the hospital it was about Penny. Three years after Alice's death... unlike his mother's terminal illness, which was identified a few years before, allowing the family to mentally prepare, it was sudden with Penny. There was no clue alerting her family that such a tragedy was going to happen.

Dez was home that Sunday evening, April 14, 1996, when she got a call informing her that one of Arthur's girls had died at the hospital. Dez very calmly went to the hospital not knowing which daughter had died. Upon arrival, she saw Bolita and Arthur. They informed her that it was Penny. Dez went into the room where Penny lay on the bed. What a very sad sight she saw, Penny laying there so peaceful, as if she were truly sleeping. Dez very slowly leaned down and kissed her on her forehead and whispered, "Penny, dear, dear Penny," then turned and left the room. Dez embraced Bolita for a long time and gave Arthur a hug and left so as not to add to the sadness with her outcries. Upon entering her car, she could not hold her sadness within any longer. It made its way out and seemed it would never end.

Eli had so much pain to think upon and hoped this Mr. Evan Kinkaid had not come to bring yet more grief upon the already devastated family.

Arthur, too, was in a hurry for morning to awaken. When it finally arrived, he left earlier than normal for work at Brant's place, knowing from the conversation he had with Brant the night before that he was to meet this Evan Kinkaid. It was as if leaving early would mean that Brant would be back sooner, and so he would be able to find out what the meeting with Mr. Kinkaid was all about.

Arthur was at Brant's place bright and early this particular morning. Before getting out of his truck, how-ever, he entertained many thoughts as to how things would go with Mr. Kinkaid. Just the thought of him hav-ing come from Paris was in itself reason to make Arthur think about himself growing up there. His thoughts were centered mainly on the years after his father had married Candace, Brant's mother.

Arthur was having good memories about all of them being together in that very big house next to a family who had three girls...three beautiful girls. The two oldest went off to boarding school, leaving the youngest one at home with her parents.

Her name was Suzanna LeAnn Caternelley.

When the two families did anything together, it always seemed that Brant and Suzanna LeAnn managed to pair off right in the middle of the bunch, and acted as if no one was in the circle around them. They laughed and laughed together to such a degree that the others laughed for the sheer delight of seeing a pair forming, a match that was sure to go somewhere. The thing was that no one knew it would progress as quickly as it did. The two of them did not want their encounters to end, such as when they were all called inside or when it was curfew, so they just went off and got married.

Brant was only fifteen and Suzanna LeAnn was a most beautiful thirteen year old. What no one knew back then, nor did anyone know today, was that Arthur had been Brant's best man. The ring Brant put on Suzanna's finger was a gift from Arthur that he secured from his own mother's jewelry box after she died. He had kept it, along with several other fine pieces of jewelry, in a safety deposit box for when he would marry. It was a ring of inheritance. Arthur told Brant not to worry about getting a ring and that he would bring one to the ceremony. When Brant saw it and realized that it was from Arthur's family inheritance, he knew even more so than when Arthur saved him from that bully that he loved him as a brother, a brother he at times wished he had while growing up.

And now, this present situation would reveal something to Brant that Arthur and Lance were aware of, but he had no knowledge. It was only a day earlier that Lance called Arthur to have a confidential talk with him about what was about to transpire between Evan Kinkaid and Brant. While in Paris, Mr. Haggerty shared information with Lance about things Brant was not aware of and that would have an impact on his life when revealed.

It was the early afternoon of the evening of the special dinner with Valtora there in Paris when Lance had gone to visit his father. While there, Mr. Haggerty asked Lance if Brant knew about what had happened to his real father, his mother's first husband, Buster Kinkaid. Lance said, "I thought Malcolm Chamberlain was Brant's real father, as I'm sure Brant thinks as well. What happened to Mr. Kinkaid?"

Mr. Haggerty answered, "Well, Lance, it's a long

story, how much time do you have?

"I'm free until tonight. I'm having dinner with Valtora."

Mr. Haggerty motioned for Lance to have a seat, and once they were both comfortable, proceeded to explain.

"Before Brant was born, Brant's mother, Candace was married to this well-to-do, pretentious person of a guy, to put it lightly. He was Buster Kinkaid."

"Sounds like a name that would suit a gun slinger."

"Well, you're not too far off. He had a string of questionably financed clubs. It was not a surprise to any who knew him when he came up missing. This was several years before I met Candace. Everyone thought that with that tragic news she would have a problem with her second pregnancy. So many catered to her during that time, and she didn't lack a thing. After she had their second baby, Brant, she needed work to support the two boys. Things got so bad for Candace that Mr. Kinkaid's mother, Jacqueline, insisted that Candace allow her to help with the boys. She allowed her to raise the older one, Evan.

Since he was already in school and loved his Grandma Jacqueline and his grandpa, whom he called Bigun, she agreed. Buster would take Evan to see them every weekend and he just took a liking to them. His Grandpa Bigun would tell everyone that Evan was their *little Isaac*, born to them in their old age, like Isaac was to Abraham and Sarah. They lived in the northern part of France and although costly to take him every weekend, it didn't matter to Buster."

"While working at one of my restaurants, Candace met Mr. Chamberlain. At the time they met, the big news circulating around was that Buster Kinkaid's body was found in the river. Candace was all shaken up about it, and her turmoil started all over again. Mr. Chamberlain was at the right place at the right time. He had the opposite disposition as Mr. Kinkaid. After more time had lapsed, they courted less than a year. People were telling Candace that Brant needed a father and she needed a husband to take care of her. They all knew Mr. Chamberlain would take care of her and even treat Brant as his own. Poor woman had so much tragedy in her life."

Mr. Haggerty shook his head as he explained these things to Lance. He continued. "They were married, and Mr. Chamberlain got her started in the business of manufacturing and marketing cologne. Her business escalated and consumed all of her time, while Mr. Chamberlain cared for his shoe business. Both of their businesses did rather well. After Mr. Chamberlain died and I found myself a widower, Candace and I just gravitated to each other, and after a short time, well, you know the rest of the story: you gained a step-brother, Brant. I always liked Brant. We hit it off from the start."

"So now I wonder if Brant is aware that Mr. Chamberlain wasn't his father and that he has a brother,

Evan, still living in France. And the man found in the river was *not* his father, Buster Kinkaid, as the news reported. Mr. Kinkaid was found in a hospital after having had a car accident that plunged him off of Whites Cliff, down into the gorge. Thank goodness a witness saw it all happen. He was taken to the Batronce` DuGaul Hospital. He was there for such a long period of time. And in the meantime, no one, I tell you, *no one* knew that man had a twin brother, not even Candace.

People wondered if *he* even knew he had a twin brother. Brant's real father, Buster Kinkaid, died only last year of a massive heart attack. I've heard that Brant's brother, Evan, will be making his way to the United States to take care of his father's business, and part of that business is to get in touch with Brant. He wanted to meet him and give him something that Mr. Kinkaid felt it important for Brant to have."

Lance was stunned. "Well, I suppose it would be better if Brant's brother tells him all of what you have told me. Has he left for the States already?"

"He was to go to New York first, as Mr. Kinkaid had interests there."

"Oh I see," said Lance, "I hope Brant takes it all well. It will be something more for him to deal with along with having found Suzanna and his children, Dezeray and Antonio. They are all so happy they have found each other. When I last saw Brant, he was indeed a happy man. I truly don't think anything can take his happiness away at this point. Not even finding out about his real father, or his having a real brother."

"I hope you're right," his father replied.

"That was some story, Dad."

BEYOND ENCOUNTERS

CHAPTER TWENTY

Evan reached into his briefcase and pulled out a long white envelope and a small package, handing them to Brant. "You might prefer to read this privately."

Brant detected a certain tone in the way Evan said those words. It sounded so caring.

"I'd rather read it now, with you here." Brant opened the envelope and began reading with no sound.

Brant,

The information in this letter that has been given to you by my son, Evan Kinkaid, is too long in coming. It is credible information and can be verified by the contents of the package he also gave you.

My name is Buster Kinkaid. Many years ago, when you were just five years old and in the living room of your home during the festival in Paris, France, I visited your mother, my wife, Candace, who at that time had married Mr. Chamberlain, the man you knew as your father all of these years.

You were hiding behind the sofa with your red cap on...

At this point, Brant felt compelled to open the small package. What he saw made him suddenly stand straight up. Flashes of his childhood raced through his mind. At first he did not want to reach inside the small box to bring out that most favorite red cap with his name on its front. He looked at it as if he wanted it to tell him what the rest of the letter was going to say. He looked at Evan as if for the first time and could not bring himself to say anything.

He had to know what else was in the letter as this was a piece of the puzzle of his past that had been brought to him by someone he did not even know. He sat down carefully and continued to read:

...and perhaps by now you are holding that very cap that has your name on the front of it. I kept it all of these years.

I came back to your house the very next day and spoke with you. I gave you a tip on hiding. I feel you will

168

remember what I told you although you were only five at the time, because it shocked you so much that you threw your cap to my feet and ran to your room. I never saw you again after that encounter.

The man who has delivered this letter to you is your full-blooded brother. Brant, I am your father. You are Brant Kinkaid.

When your mother was pregnant with you I was with the wrong kind of people. It cost me in a very big way, as you may understand to some degree. My twin brother was found in the Canal River and everyone assumed he was me. He was on his way to visit me in Montreal, Canada. Little did I know, he was caught up in business transactions that cost him dearly, his life.

I didn't find out about this until I was able to come out of hiding. I, too, had been living under threat to my life. It took all of five years in staying hidden away in Canada, distancing myself from your mother and your brother, before I could return. My parents, your grandparents, Bigun and Jacqueline, helped your mother out with your brother, Evan, by raising him in northern France.

I plead with you, please hold nothing against Evan. He is your brother. He is innocent and I beg you not to hold any harsh feelings toward him that you may have against me.

I have only myself to blame that your mother married Mr. Chamberlain, the man you looked to as your fa-

ther. You and I did meet that one time, and I did carry you in my thoughts until now, as I know I am losing ground. I wanted you to know.

That day when you were hiding, before I knew you were there, and while talking to your mother, I told her that you should know. I couldn't press the issue as I had brought it upon not only myself, but also upon you and Candace.

Please forgive me son.

Your father,
Buster Kinkaid"

At that point Brant dropped the hand that was holding the letter and buried his face in his other hand and cried as he had never before, as he did indeed recall those few words uttered by his father. Sobbing, Brant muttered the phrase, "…the boy should know, the boy should know."

Only three persons heard those words that day and they were the words Brant would bring from the crevice of his mind all these years.

"That man in the living room was my biological father who had been mistakenly reported dead? That body found in the river was wrongly presumed to have been that of my real father? My father's twin brother was mistaken as my father? How in the world could that be? Didn't anyone investigate the dead man?"

He barraged Evan with question after question.

Brant now knew that after some time had passed after the discovery of the body in the river, his mother, Candace, married Mr. Chamberlain. From the time Brant could say *Daddy,* he looked at Mr. Chamberlain as his real father, something that did not set well with Buster Kinkaid. The heated confrontation in the living room that day, all those years ago, between Candace and Mr. Kinkaid, found little Brant behind the sofa.

Evan placed his hand firmly upon Brant's shoulder in an effort to comfort him and Brant welcomed such an emotional gesture. He was so moved that he literally fell upon Evan. At that point Evan wrapped his arms around Brant, and the both of them cried together.

"I know this is unbelievable to you, and you have many questions," said Evan.

Brant managed to say to Evan, "I just couldn't put this piece to the puzzle all these years. I felt there was something, I had no idea it was to this magnitude. Was he ill for a long time?"

"No, it happened suddenly. It was a heart attack."

"Thank you for this," said Brant as he raised the letter.

"I don't have much to say at the moment, yet there's so much I want to know. I know you need to get back, my wife said you wanted to get back to New York to take care of his interests there."

"Yes, I do have to get back, Brant, but I will return.

Mr. Haggerty, your step-father, was a great help to me in finding you. Now that I know where you are, I will return, I promise, just as I promised Father that I would get these things to you. After everything is sorted out, I will have to meet with you again, as our father was a very wealthy man, and he did not forget about either of us."

Eli gave Brant all the room and time he needed to absorb what he observed to be a very moving moment with Evan. It all felt right, so Eli just patiently waited until Brant wanted to share.

Brant, in a most heartfelt way said to Evan, "Evan, I can't begin to tell you how much your visit has eased my state of mind. I have been puzzled for so many years. You have provided the missing piece, although the puzzle of my life appeared to have been complete when I finally found Suzanna and our children. And now, with all of this, how is it possible to even begin to thank you for carrying out our father's requests?"

"You need say no more, Brant. From the letter you just read, you have a favorable attitude toward our father as I myself do. Knowing that is gratitude enough for me."

Brant embraced Evan once again. As they stood to leave, Brant motioned to Eli to join them. After revealing Evan's identity, Brant said, "Well, Eli, this is the last of what my mind has held on to from the past, and now I am satisfied knowing that the journey is indeed over."

Eli was grateful. "Thank you for allowing me to be part of this most important experience. I feel closer to you, more than ever now, Brant."

Eli embraced Brant while Evan looked on in an emotional way, after which Eli turned to Evan and said, "It's a pleasure to meet you once again, but this time as Uncle Evan. My wife, your niece, will be happy to know there is one more member to add to the family, which will make for a longer book that she's thinking about writing. I have a feeling that after she finds out what has just happened she'll be moved to get started right away."

All the while Eli was telling Evan Kinkaid these things, he thought about all the names his wife had now. He would have to go home and say with the biggest smile, "Hello Dezeray Payton, Chamberlain, Kinkaid, Ortello".

"The pleasure is mine explicitly, Eli. I hope to meet your wife and the rest of the family on a return trip."

After Evan left the restaurant, Brant said to Eli, "This is the end of my journey. I was doubtful it was really over, after I had found my family. Today I no longer have doubts. This is something I have wondered about since I was five. It makes all the sense in the world. I remember it as if it were yesterday. I must go to Suzanna and let her know all of this. She is worried; I can feel it, as I'm sure Dez is. You want to let Dez know what this newcomer wanted, don't you?"

"Yes, Brant, yes, I do! Let's go, I'm eager to talk with Dez."

BEYOND ENCOUNTERS

CHAPTER TWENTY-ONE

When Brant got near the house, Suzanna was outside and from a distance, Brant saw her at the easel he had put at the gazebo. Her back was to the entrance to keep the early morning's blaring sun from her face. She looked ever so lovely, as if time had stood still during all the years they were apart. Brant loved her so much and the tears he caught in his handkerchief showed just how heartfelt that love was. And now, feeling complete after the revelation Evan brought him, his love for her had grown deeper since that day, so many years ago when he kissed her before she left the house that morning for her

flight attendant job at Charles De Gaulle Airport.

He smiled as he parked, and sat and watched her paint. He wanted to savor the moment. He wanted many more moments as this one, to look at Suzanna LeAnn with the idea of caring for her as he never had before; to reminisce about the two of them; to finally feel complete, knowing that things do not always turn out as favorable for others. As he watched her, he could only imagine the turmoil she had gone through in her life, and vowed to do his utmost to spare her any further pain.

He reflected on the day he got back from Cranbrook after his long hoped for encounter with Suzanna, spurred on by the letter that Kathryn had written to Tese and that he had discovered when he took care of Tese's things after her death. He got out of the car taking his father's letter and the small box into the house. He then retrieved Tese's letter and went to sit on his porch swing to read it. So happy that he had come by that letter from Kathryn, he read it again so as to mull over a few passages that stuck out in his mind.

Dear Tese,

I hope this letter finds you in the best of health. Donald is well, and other than this bronchitis I get off and on, all is going good here. Dezeray is doing just fine. We both love her as our own.

I'm writing this time to tell you that I'm not certain Suzanna is getting any better in the institution she committed herself to. They found she hasn't been taking her medication.

I've been taking current pictures of Dez to her and pictures you send me of Antonio and Brant, but, there's nothing that's bringing her around to want to leave that place. I just don't know Tese. I feel so bad for her, yet I'm so happy she and Brant allowed Donald and me to bring Dez here and raise her.

I haven't told Dezeray about Suzanna LeAnn, and at times I grapple with the thought of telling her, but I still feel this is the best way, Tese. No one knows where Suzanna is except you and me and please let it stay that way.

Before she got worse, she told me that she wanted to get better so she could once again be with Antonio, Dez and Brant."

At that point, Brant stopped reading and thought if only he had known the years previous to his finding the letter where Suzanna had gone, Suzanna could have had her desire for being with the family sooner. He continued:

She's in good hands and that's the way it'll have to stay. I just wanted to give you an update, although it wasn't a good one. Please Tese, keep what I tell you safe and tell no one. It's the way Suzanna would want it.

Brant could not help but reason upon the thought that 'it was the way *Kathryn* wanted it'. He tried hard not to harbor resentment, but it ate at him because for years he was robbed of the joy he could have had with Suzanna. So to put the letter in the past and spare the ill feelings that may come about from anyone else getting hold of it, Brant destroyed it. He felt it served its purpose, a purpose that ended the journey in search of his long-lost love.

After returning from Cranbrook that day, not only did he get her a car, but, when he first saw her out on the grounds at Cranbrook painting at the easel, he was determined to make a place for her to paint when she was released to go home with him. The place he chose was near one of the lakes on their land, not too far from the house. At the mouth of the lake there stood the gazebo, and as she now stood there making delicate strokes on a canvas, he thought how beautiful a painting this very scene would make.

She felt his presence, and turning in his direction, she held up the paint brush and beckoned for him to come her way. Before Brant reached Suzanna, her brush was put away, and she had taken a seat on the bench under a huge live oak tree close to the gazebo. They sat there together while Brant related what the newcomer to Hallettsville had brought him. The sigh of relief from Suzanna after hearing the whole story was like a signal for Brant to embrace her. And embrace her he did.

Dez told Eli that she would begin writing about everything that had happened, now that the other shoe had fallen and all pieces of the puzzle were in place and she would begin writing as they were leaving Hallettsville for their vacation in the mountains of New Mexico where she hoped the two of them would get snowed in.

Eli arranged for that trip to take place and all of what they had hoped for... happened. They had their first snowed-in experience on Camelot Mountain. They were able to hear the quietness that Dezeray had written about in her poem "Quiet Nights". It was a most unique scene, coupled with the muffled sound all around, with the occasional crackling of a branch heavily overlaid with ice. As for the snowflakes, not one was exactly alike in their splendor.

The other vacationers, along with Dez and Eli, were informed of what the order of the snowed-in evening was to be like, in regards to eating, if anyone so desired. They were invited to prepare a covered dish in their condominium and take it to the main dining area for a shared meal.

CHAPTER TWENTY-TWO

That two-week vacation turned out to be a needed rest for them because of what lay ahead. Six months after Penny died, Dez found herself in a situation with her mother that would not have a good ending.

Dez vividly remembered all of what took place with her mother.

One day Suzanna called Dezeray to come over because she wanted to talk with her.

"What's wrong, Mother?" Dez asked anxiously.

"I'd rather you come over, Dear. We can talk when you get here."

That was an unusual call, Dez thought to herself as she drove to her mother's house. When she got there, Suzanna was sitting in the living room and looked somewhat worried.

It was around the time that a convention was going

to be held at the Astrodome in Houston, Texas, about a week away. Suzanna began the conversation with Dezeray.

"Dezeray, I'm concerned about blood that I see in the toilet after I use the bathroom."

"Mother, let me call Dr. Downing's office and let her see you. That doesn't sound good at all."

"That's what I thought, Dez, but, I want to go on the trip and get the results when I get home."

"Okay, Mother, that's okay. Let me use your phone and call for an appointment right now."

"I'd appreciate it if you would set it up, Dezeray. You're going to miss Adreanna when she goes to New York. I'm so glad you're here with me."

"I'm glad to be here with you, Mother. And yes, you're right; I know I'll miss Adreanna when she goes to New York. We'll keep in close contact. She'll only be three hours and a minute away."

"Three hours and a minute?"

"Yes, that's what the pilot said on Continental Airlines when we went to visit Tory. He said the fight was 'three hours and a minute'."

As they were talking about how close Adreanna would be, the telephone was ringing at the doctor's office. The secretary answered and Dez asked to speak to Jeanette.

"Sure, one moment please."

"This is Jeanette."

"Jeanette, how are you?"

"I'm doing okay."

"That's good. This is Dezeray. I'm at my mom's house and she just told me that she has seen blood in the toilet when she goes to the bathroom. She says there are clots, and I want Dr. Downing to check her."

"Can you bring her in now?"

"Yes, I can, we'll be right there."

Brant, Suzanna LeAnn and Dezeray went to the doctor's office. Dr. Downing attended Suzanna with the same loving care as she had always done with Jake. The doctor told Suzanna that she would call when the results were in.

As Suzanna and Brant were going to the car, Dezeray told Jeanette that her mother did not want to know the results until after she got back from a trip that had been planned earlier in the year. It would be a trip that Eli and Dezeray would accompany Brant and Suzanna.

Later that week, the doctor's office called Dezeray to inform her of the result of the tests. To Dezeray's dismay and great sadness, the news was bad. Suzanna had uterine cancer and would need surgery with radiation therapy follow up. Jeanette told Dezeray that Dr. Downing would contact the oncology doctor in San Antonio, but that she would make all of the arrangements for them. She also informed Dez that there were accommodations in the area of the hospital where relatives assisting the patient could stay for prolonged stays.

Dez informed Eli. The two of them were aware of the bad news throughout the trip.

When they arrived back to Hallettsville, and on a morning when the sunrise appeared the most beautiful in all of the history of their watching it from their homes, Dezeray accompanied Suzanna LeAnn and Brant to the doctor's office for what would be the beginning of another journey. This time Suzanna and Brant would travel it together with their children, Dezeray and Antonio, and with all of the love and support of their reunited family.

Antonio was consulted for the second opinion and confirmed the diagnosis.

The majestic sunrise that could be seen this morning would soon be the sunset of Suzanna LeAnn's life.

The most striking thing about the whole discovery of Suzanna LeAnn's cancer was her serene disposition. She remained ever so calm throughout it all, never one bitter word, ever. One would think it impossible for a person to learn about such tragic news and not react in at least one irrational way. This was not the case with Suzanna LeAnn.

Sometime later, with radiation treatment behind her, Suzanna was home. Brant was there. Dezeray was also there visiting them. Suzanna did not appear just right to Dezeray. It appeared that Suzanna's motor skills were slow. Right away Dezeray called for an ambulance and it appeared in a matter of minutes, although Brant's home was located outside the city limits of Hallettsville.

Suzanna was transported to Hallettsville's Medical Center. The emergency room doctor noted right away that Suzanna was in the middle of having a stroke and administered the medications to stop it, thereby sparing Suzanna the debilitating losses normally associated with a stroke.

Not much later, while in the local hospital recuperating from the stroke, a spur of some kind began pinching the back of Suzanna's neck, causing her great pain. An ambulance ride one hundred miles away to Houston, Texas, got her to the hospital where a procedure was performed followed by an operation on her neck. It was a success. Before the operation however, Suzanna LeAnn would cry out in pain. Pain medication did not seem to suffice.

At night, beside her mother's bed, Dezeray prayed that her mother not suffer, not be in pain. Antonio got to the Houston hospital to help Dezeray with their mother and to attend to their mother's needs. Massaging her neck became the order of the day because it soothed her. Antonio James, the middle name Dez would call Antonio at times like these, would for hours massage his mother's neck until his back hurt. Dezeray would then take over for him until he could resume comforting her with such tender loving care. Antonio James would look at Dezeray and shake his head as he felt the pain their mother was going through, holding his own back as he massaged his mother's neck.

It was the day before her neck surgery. Brant was just as loving to Suzanna as he lightly kissed her cheek each morning and evening as he would come and go from the hospital.

On the day of the surgery the doctor explained the procedure and all went well. Suzanna was able to recuperate at the hospital and do rehab right there at the hospital.

The Physical Therapist came in each morning for the following days. Eli made a trip from Hallettsville to pick up Brant and take him back home to obtain outfits for Suzanna's moving to another floor for more intense physical therapy.

One particular morning, Brant and Eli left the hospital after Brant kissed Suzanna on her forehead and Eli kissed Dez. Dezeray cared for her mother's usual morning routine and then fixed her hair. *What a beautiful woman*, Dez thought to herself.

Dez said, "Wow, don't you look pretty, Mother."

Suzanna replied, "But my lipstick, I won't ever be caught without my lipstick."

Dez applied the red lipstick onto her mother's already naturally lined lips, and told her mother, "Do you think I'll get that natural line around my lips like yours? I like that; you don't even have to put liner on your lips."

Suzanna smiled, "I see a line around your lips, and you didn't put it there."

Dezeray looked in the mirror near the bed and agreed with her and said, "I think you're right, but, yours are prettier than mine."

At that point the physical therapist came in and helped Suzanna with her regular exercises. Dezeray left the bedside of her mother and walked the therapist to the door, closed it behind the nurse and walked back over to her mother. As she neared the bed, Dezeray saw her mother's beautiful face. As her mother smiled at her, Suzanna's eyes rolled to the back.

Dezeray screamed, "Mother, what's the matter!?" Dezeray frantically pushed the call button and called out, "Come in here quick! My mother needs help! Hurry! It's an emergency!"

She ran and opened the door and screamed down the hallway, "Hurry up and come in here! My mother needs help!" The words were barely out of her mouth before nurses were in the room. The room became so filled with people. Through the noisy bustle, Dez could hear a male doctor say, "Mrs. Chamberlain, breathe! Breathe, Mrs. Chamberlain!"

When all of the nurses flooded into the room, Dezeray crawled onto the bay window so she could get a glimpse of her mother above the heads of all the medical people. When Dezeray heard the doctor loudly tell her mother to breathe, Dezeray yelled out, "Breathe, Mother! They want you to breathe!"

At that point Dezeray heard someone yell. "Take

her out of here! Take her out of here now!"

"No!" said Dezeray very sternly. "I want to be here!"

Then a very gentle hand was on Dezeray's shoulder and a calm voice said, "Honey, we can help your mother much better if you come outside with me."

Her soft spoken words compelled Dezeray to move past the bed, looking tearfully in the direction of her mother. Once outside, before it appeared, the noise of the defibrillator could be heard being pushed very quickly into her room.

It was not but a few seconds it seemed, but Dezeray later learned that an hour or more had passed between the time she was taken from the room until the doctor walked down the hall and to where the nurse had taken her. The doctor apologized. "I am so sorry. I am totally shocked that we lost your mother."

"What!" exclaimed Dezeray, "Lost her? My mother is dead?"

"Yes, we couldn't save her."

"What happened!?"

"All of what happened to your mother happened instantaneously."

That word stuck with Dezeray. "Instantaneously." The doctor told the nurse to take Dezeray to the lounge and he would be in to talk with her about it further, but at the moment he had to attend to her mother and arrange things.

The nurse took Dezeray to the lounge and comforted her with kind words. Dez kept asking what happened. The nurse said that the doctor would be able to answer that and assured her that he would return soon.

When she calmed down somewhat, Dezeray called family and before long she was surrounded. She called Hallettsville. Eli and Brant had not even arrived there to gather clothes for Suzanna. When they did get word, they were back at the Houston hospital right away.

Brant hugged Dezeray and they both cried. Eli then held Dezeray as she was silent.

Sitting on the front porch when he got back to Hallettsville from Houston, Brant listened to the songs that he and Suzanna had listened to. He then went to the telephone and called Evan to tell him about Suzanna LeAnn's death. Evan expressed his sorrow and said he was coming to the United States for her memorial service.

Evan's granddaughter, Tamaral, accompanied him to the United States to finalize their father's will. While there, Brant and Evan talked.

"Brant, after I got word about Suzanna LeAnn's death, I hurried father's business accountants to finish up the paperwork so when I came to her memorial service we could take care of the finances connected to his will. No doubt you are totally unaware of our father's assets."

Buster Kinkaid's parents always kept Evan informed about his father, never letting too much time lapse before telling him why he was living with them.

Evan, speaking to Brant, told him of conversations between him and his grandfather, Bigun. "I used to tell my grandfather that I remembered my dad. I remember him putting me on his shoulders when we arrived, and when we would get to the bridge over the stream, he carried me across to Bigun's house. Halfway across we would stop and wait until the deer would come out of hiding. We did that every time we came from visiting mother. I never forgot it and never will."

"Then I wondered after I was older, why Dad had become a sad man when he used to be happy. I told Bigun that I could almost pinpoint when he changed. Before that terrible mistaken identity, he had gone to Paris happy, but when he returned, he had changed, as if his world was shaken. I know now he had found out while on that trip to Paris that mother had remarried and you were being raised by another man."

Dad told me everything when he thought I would understand, about how he felt about that man who was taking good care of you and Mother. He thought it best to stay out of your life after that heated conversation in the living room of your house. When I wanted to get in touch with you, information turned up that your step-father had died and mother had married Mr. Haggerty. You had married this very young girl - not that you were even old enough for marriage. Before long, we heard that you were a father. After a while, we lost track of you. I started a family, and then my first grand-daughter, Tamaral was born. We call her Tammy."

"She now wants to move here to the United States. She's read about the opportunities New York has to offer. Her mother and father are a bit skeptical, but they are determined not to stand in the way of what could be her dream becoming a reality. So when she heard I was coming back here, she heard opportunity knock, but the family knows no one in the States."

Brant interrupted. "Now hold on Evan. It's my turn to speak. That is just not true at all. My journey was hard and long in getting my family together. I thought I *had,* until the day I walked through the doors of the restaurant and saw you. Now the journey you undertook to find me, your own flesh and blood, has turned up a family you haven't known. My step brother, Lance, lives in New York, so does my grandson, Tory, and his sister, Adreanna. She's about your age, Tammy, and since you want to move there, you have family that will be ready to help you."

Evan was pleased. "Her parents and the rest of the family will be happy about all of this, Brant. Thank you for sharing your family."

"Well, it's the right thing to do, Evan," Brant said matter-of-factly. "It's a great thing to have family," he said as he shed tears in his handkerchief over Suzanna

LeAnn.

Suzanna's remains were buried on October 16, 1996 in the family's cemetery plot in Cuero, Texas.

"We're together now, Brant, you, me, our families. We're together now," that thought seemed to comfort Brant.

After their stay in Hallettsville, Evan and his granddaughter made preparations to leave.

"When it's time for Tammy to come here, we'll call you and go from there."

"That's good, Evan," said Brant. "In fact, I'll be calling Lance later tonight and I will inform him about your granddaughter."

"Thank you again, Brant. We had better be on our way."

Brant and Evan embraced as they had on his first visit.

BEYOND ENCOUNTERS

CHAPTER TWENTY-THREE

Five years have passed and the majority of the first encounters are thriving with interesting things going on. However, the saddest encounter was yet ahead.

Dez was determined to finish the novel she had started the day she and Eli went on vacation to New Mexico. It would be a detailed story about her father and all that she learned from him on a regular basis. She would strive to learn all about this man who appeared in the Internet Café in Hallettsville one afternoon while she and Eli were having a romantic lunch. This would be a story about his quest to bring his family back together.

During that snowy trip, as was always the case,

Dez was looking at the calendar planning the next vacation *before* they arrived home. It would be a trip to New York to visit Adreanna and Tory, and would prove to be one they would never forget as long as they both lived.

Once again Arelius found himself in charge of the feed store. Over the years he had proven himself to be a very dependable and very business-like young man.

After Eli and Dez got to New York they unpacked and were finally situated in the garage apartment that a friend of Tory's, Mike Mattontou, allowed them to use.

Mike took everyone out to dinner. It was Tuesday night, October 5th, 1999. When Eli and Dez got back to the apartment, Dez thought she had better call Jake and give him all the telephone numbers where he could reach them if the need arose. Thinking he was probably with his friends, because she got no answer, she thought calling early the next morning would be a better time since he went in to do voluntary work at the Eagle Pass Duncan Hospital. Calling again in the morning would be good and she would talk with him then and give him the number to the garage apartment.

Up early Wednesday morning, October 6th, 1999, Dez called Jake's apartment and again got no answer. There was a slight worry on Dez's part, because in the past, through her persistence, she was always able to put her finger on the location of the children no matter where they happened to be. This would be no different she thought. It would be just a matter of time before she would talk with Jake. Every hour that passed proved her wrong as there was still no contact.

Her next thought was to call the hospital to see if he had made it for his volunteer assignment. The voice on the other end of the phone sounded worried. "No, ma'am, Jake hasn't come in for work yet. He's usually here by 1 p.m. I'll call his apartment after we hang up and if I get him, I'll let him know you're trying to reach him," said the receptionist.

"Thank you very much, I'd appreciate that," said Dez as she thought to perhaps see if he had gone in as a patient for pain. He had not. Now, after being unsuccessful, the only thing Dez thought about at this point was to find him. *Was his ringer off?* Dez thought.

After leaving the apartment to go to Brooklyn, Dez would call at every telephone booth she saw on Montague Street. Eli did not allow his concern to show. He knew that if he did, Dez would worry even more.

Dez thought they should call the manager of Jake's apartment complex. A man by the name of Keith answered and identified himself as the acting manager, and said that Jo Alder was no longer working there. Dez asked Keith had he seen Jake lately.

He said he saw his car the night before while he was doing security check, which was Tuesday night. Dez told Keith that she and Eli were worried and if he would go check in Jake's apartment to see if he was okay. He said okay and to call back in thirty minutes.

Dez and Adreanna called back to the office in the thirty minutes, but there was no answer. They went into a hotel on Montague Street to wait for Eli and Tory to meet back up with them at six p.m.

While waiting in the hotel, Dez went to a small triangular marbled shelf to use the courtesy phone to call Jake's apartment again. A man answered the phone.

"Who are you?" he questioned.

Dez was surprised, "Who are *you*?"

The man then asked, "Are you Jake's mother?"

Dez was very confused, "Yes, and I'd like to speak with Keith. Is he there?"

"Yes, he is here, but Keith can't speak with you at this time, ma'am. I'm detective Lopez, and I'm so sorry to have to inform you, but your son Jake has passed away here... in his bed."

"What!" Dez cried out, with her voice going throughout the hotel lobby. "I want to speak with Keith!" demanded Dez in a tone heard by Adreanna sitting on the sofa not too far from Dez.

"Ma'am, the Justice of the peace pronounced your son dead at 3:25pm today and has ordered an autopsy for him. May we have permission from you to have this done?"

Dez asked, "What happened?"

Detective Lopez said, "It appears that your son took a

shower, got in bed, pulled the covers up to his chin and went to sleep. He died in his sleep. There's no trauma on his face; the air conditioner is on so he appears just as when he went to sleep. His radio is barely audible and his TV is on. We don't suspect foul play, but a person as young as your son, well, we really need your permission to do the autopsy. May we have it?"

"How long has he been…" Dez could not finish the question.

The officer responded, "I feel it's been two days."

Dez cried out, "No! Two days!" and broke down there at the phone.

Adreanna was at her mother's side, "Mother, what's wrong?"

Dez did not respond to Adreanna, but she knew something was terribly wrong. She massaged her mother's neck and said, "Take a deep breath, Mother."

She did, and then told her that Jake had died in his apartment in Eagle Pass.

Dez told Officer Lopez that she would call him back in twenty minutes, after she had spoken with Jake's father.

The detective said he had Dez's other son on the other line.

Dez was surprised and asked, "Tory"?

"No - Arelius."

Dez weakly asked, "Does Arelius know?"

"Yes, he does and he has been very helpful about

Jake."

Dez said, "I'm going to talk with my husband, Eli, and we'll call you back."

Adreanna, Dez's right arm of support at that particular time, with tear filled eyes, remained strong for her mother as they went to another location in Brooklyn a few blocks over, on Columbia Heights, to see if Eli and Tory were there. They were not. While going to Columbia Heights Street, Dez noticed a phone booth and thought she would call to give permission for the autopsy. She thought for sure Eli would agree to it. Before calling the officer, Dez called Arelius.

"How's everything, Arelius?"

"Fine," said Arelius in an unsure voice that Dez detected.

"Did you speak to someone from Eagle Pass just a while ago?"

"Yes, Mother, so you're aware of what happened with Jake?"

"Yes, son, I am. How are you? Are you okay?"

"Yes, I'm okay. How are you and Daddy? Does Adreanna know? And Tory, does he know?"

"Adreanna knows, and she's okay too, but we haven't touched bases with Daddy or Tory yet. Arelius, I'm going to go ahead and give them permission to do the autopsy. They want to do one."

"Okay, I feel Daddy would agree to it."

"Thank you for that, Arelius. I love you, take care,

and be strong. Why don't you call your grandfather and Uncle Arthur to let them know. They'll be there for you, we're so far away. I wish we were there right now. We'll be in touch with you."

"Okay, I will, Mother. I'll be okay."

Before hanging up, so as not to be left alone with what Keith had asked him, Arelius said, "Oh, Mother, Keith asked me for permission to dispose of Jake's mattress. I asked him why he was asking me that. After he told me what happens at death, I gave him permission."

"You did well, Arelius, you did very well."

Arelius could not find it within himself to stick out his not-so-little chest at his mother's praising of him. It just did not feel right to do so this time. They said their good-byes and Dez called Jake's apartment once again.

She found herself in the saddest situation she ever faced in her life.

While Dez was on the telephone with Detective Lopez, Eli and Tory came up the street talking and smiling. Adreanna would never forget her daddy's face as he and Tory approached them. When he saw his wife's face as she spoke to the detective, he knew something awful had happened and his smile disappeared.

Dez told them that Jake had died in his sleep. Fran

and her sister, Karly were with them. They all huddled on the street and cried and cried. Koin, a friend of Tory's, passed by. Tory told him what had happened. Then another friend of Tory's passed by, Mr. Dugay. Eli told him what had happened. Very compassionately he said, "Let me know what we can do for you all while you're here in New York."

They all went upstairs in one of the buildings on Columbia Heights to continue to make necessary phone calls.

The first call made was to the Memorial Funeral Home in Eagle Pass, Texas, informing them of their decision to cremate Jake's body after it had undergone the autopsy in San Antonio. The secretary at the funeral home said they would fax all the paperwork needed and instructed them to fill out and sign them for cremation and for the death certificate. They would call on Mr. Dugay for help with this. Things were going so fast.

Dez kept in touch with Arelius during the remainder of their trip, and she and Eli handled everything that was possible while so far away.

All the necessary papers were sent early the next day. Dez and Eli thought that, since Arelius was with Brant and all of his relatives and friends, they would stay with Adreanna and Tory for a few days and then they would all fly back to Texas together for Jake's memorial service.

When Eli and Dez went to get the faxed materials,

two more of Tory's friends, Tom and Al, greeted them with a sympathy card with many condolences written on the card from more of Tory's friends. How encouraging and strengthening that was for the two of them, which in turn made them strong not only for the ordeal yet ahead but more importantly to be a strong support for the children.

Eli felt so encouraged that he decided to handle the arrangements himself. After Dez asked him if he was absolutely certain that he could do it, and he firmly told her yes, she knew he could and she would provide all the support he needed to accomplish it.

They arrived back in Texas and all went as planned.

After some time had passed, Dez and Eli realized that they had not, as of yet, fully dealt with their dear son's death. Their lives had been filled with the functions of day-to-day living, with running a business and caring for family responsibilities to such an extent that they had been able to avoid really facing their grief. But almost suddenly, it demanded their attention. Dez spoke with Eli about going to Cape Cod, Massachusetts and how she wanted to walk out on the jetties and just sit and think about how she would write about Jake's death and remembering the things that lead up to finding out about it.

Eli was very agreeable, knowing it would do her good. He thought to himself on many occasions how seemingly well Dez had handled Jake's death, and wondered if one day it would hit her and she would have to face reality.

When the time came for Dez to make the trip to Cape Cod, she spoke with Eli in detail about the inward feelings that had never surfaced about Jake's death. As she shared her feelings with Eli, her voice began to tremble for the first time while talking about Jake. It seemed that now was the time to allow what had been bottled up for the past four years to well up to the point of overflowing. She finally cried long and hard, with no one other than Eli and her in the house at the time.

She cried in Eli's arms until she fell asleep. He held her all night. As Eli was lying there holding Dez ever so gently and stroking her hair, he recalled Dez's rapport with all of Jake's friends the day of his memorial service. It was as if it was not her son who had died, but someone else, and she was consoling all of the relatives and all of his friends who had come great distances to his memorial service. He remembered, too, that she was the very last one to sit, just before the memorial talk started. She made sure all were seated first. Although Jake had many close friends, there was one in particular who had arrived unaccompanied, Rachel. Dez took her to a seat right next to her seat so she would not be alone.

And now with this outward outpouring of grief

from Dez indicating her acceptance that Jake was indeed gone, Eli was all the more ready for her to go about healing in the way she felt she needed to.

"If going away to Cape Cod would aid in your healing process, my love, then let it be done," he softly whispered before closing his own tear-filled eyes, as he thought about their unfortunate, most terrible loss.

BEYOND ENCOUNTERS

CHAPTER TWENTY-FOUR

Jake's family had kept close emotionally during the past years, each supporting the other through what seemed to be a never ending effort to cope. Additionally, with the exception of Adreanna, everyone had a special someone when those moments of private grief were best shared alone.

Adreanna, however, would not remain unattached very long, as Lance was determined that she meet his step-mother's son, Edward Malinfe`. Before Lance and Edward met, Lance had arranged that Adreanna interview with one of his clients whose office was in the Met Life building, in the heart of New York City. He ran the computer support department of what turned out to be the same law firm where Edward practiced. Adreanna had the skills necessary and she was brought on board as a support technician. She only worked part-time which made a coincidental encounter with Edward a most unlikely event. Lance had already mentioned to her that a certain young man that he knew was eager to meet her. None of them realized then that the two of them had already met.

It was on a Friday. While Edward enjoyed a sip of water at the water fountain, Adreanna stepped out of the elevator on his left. She was responding to a trouble call from an office on the fourteenth floor to help with an unresponsive computer. When Eddie finished drinking, there stood Adreanna outside his office door. He watched her for a while as she read what appeared to be a book. He was stunned at this girl's beauty, confident that there was none in the entire world to match her.

Adreanna had stepped out of the elevator, book in hand, and face in book. While still reading, she knocked on the office door from where the call had come from. After knocking a fourth time, a few moments passed and she thought she should pay attention to her surroundings since she had too long been engrossed in her mother's novel and now aware of Eddie's presence. Her eyes met his as she turned around, and for a moment she was thoroughly embarrassed. It was a moment that she hoped he did not notice as she gained her composure and straightened her relaxed body, giving him her full attention. When she saw his amused expression, she realized he had not missed a thing and her embarrassment quickly faded. Refusing to give him the upper hand, she turned back to the door and knocked even harder, as if someone was then sure to answer.

Eddie was now standing next to her. "Hello, would you like to go inside this office?"

Adreanna was curt. "Yes, someone called about their computer."

"And you're here to fix it?"

What Adreanna wanted to reply was, "No, I'm just in the neighborhood and since I have nothing better to do I'm here banging on doors." But what she actually said was, "Yes, I was going to give it a try."

As soon as Adreanna said the word *try*, Eddie exclaimed, "Whoa! You're from the south!"

"Is that a statement or a question?" she quipped.

"Ok, ok, I take that back… You're a New Yorker!"

They both laughed.

"See, that's just why!" said Adreanna, "Oh well, I've followed up on this call, no one is here, that's their loss. I have to get back to my post."

Eddie didn't want her to leave yet. "But that poor guy will be disappointed if he doesn't get his computer fixed. Perhaps he just left his office for a drink of water."

"That could very well be true," said Adreanna as she quickly assessed the situation realizing that the office must have belonged to him.

"Poor *guy*?" asked Adreanna, raising her eyebrows

in his direction.

"Yes, a *guy* occupies this office." His arms were now crossed across his chest.

"I just a few minutes ago spoke with a person from this very floor, and it certainly was a female asking IT to send someone up to fix her computer," said Adreanna, feigning confusion.

"A female?" asked Eddie in a serious tone.

"Well, the voice sounded like a female."

"What name did she give you?"

"You sure are inquisitive," said Adreanna, gloating in her approaching victory. It was Etta Malinfe`."

Smiling, Eddie said, "It's *Eddie* Malinfe`."

"Oh, I sure thought I heard Etta!" Her smile revealed she was joking with him.

"Alright," said Eddie, "I think I've been found out. You already know my name. And you? What's yours, if I may ask?"

"You may ask," Adreanna said in a playful tone then stood and waited.

Eddie went along with the game. "May I please know what your name is, Ma'am?

"Adreanna Ortello." She bowed her head ever so slightly.

"Well," he replied, one arm bent across his belt line, slight bend in his waist, "It was a pleasure to meet you. I certainly hope this poor guy will have access to his computer again. I would appreciate it if you'd give it your best shot."

"Nice meeting you as well. Now if I can get into this office that I've nearly banged the door down, I'll be happy to fix your computer."

"If you fix it, I'll treat you to dinner in the cafeteria."

"Okay. I'll have the Texas chicken fried steak, and thank you."

"You said I was inquisitive - well I have a few more questions for you since you're so sure I'll be treating you to lunch. I like that - a girl sure of herself."

After Adreanna reset the password on his computer he asked if she would be interested in attempting to beat him in a game or two of tic-tac-toe. She could not resist the challenge.

Anxious for Eddie's introduction to his niece, Lance reserved a large table at his restaurant, Le`Shatonique, for a Saturday night gathering of several of his family and friends. He included his assistant, Christopher Jay Michael, out of appreciation for his continued excellent service.

He also invited his nephew, Tory, who requested that he be able to bring Fran. Lance agreed, but only after interrogating Tory in great detail about the relationship, how he met her, where she was from, how long he had known her until Tory was breathless with exasperation.

"Uncle Lance, can she just come with me?"

"Absolutely! Please bring her!" He admired Tory for asking first.

When extending the invitation to Eddie, Lance included Eddie's sister, Olivia. She also lived in New York, and Lance remembered Eddie commenting that she owned an art gallery in SoHo. He hoped to see Adreanna find an outlet for her interest in art, and perhaps a willing spirit in Olivia. Olivia could be helpful to Adreanna in her pursuit of an art career.

Adreanna arrived at the restaurant as planned, bringing her cousin Tammy, recently arriving in New York from Paris. They both took their seats at the table where almost everyone was already seated.

Last to arrive were Eddie and Olivia. As they greeted the group, Adreanna's surprise was evident.

"Eddie Malinfe`! Why are *you* here!?"

Lance was pleased. "Evidently you two already know each other."

"Yes," said Eddie. "We have met."

"I had no idea this was the person you had told me about, Uncle Lance," said Adreanna. Relieved as she was, it was difficult for her to hide her smile.

"No problem, Adreanna, I'm glad you met Eddie."

As they settled in their seats Eddie was quick to introduce Olivia.

"Everyone, this is my sister, Olivia."

All said hello and before long they were enjoying

their meal, the table was noisy with conversation.

Adreanna and Olivia discussed their mutual interest in art. Eddie watched Adreanna closely, causing Lance to wonder just how long they had known each other, especially when he observed Eddie's obvious interest. Lance engaged Eddie in a conversation about the how's and when's of their meeting.

After dinner Tammy approached Christopher Jay Michael and asked, "Do I have to call you what my Uncle Lance called you, 'Christopher Jay Michael', each time I say your name?"

"You can just call me JC."

"And not CJ?" asked Tammy.

"No, I'm around a lot of CJ's and they're all girls. So I've stuck with JC all this time."

"I like your whole name, but I'll take you up on calling you JC."

"Did I understand you correctly?" smiled JC. "Did you say you were going to call me? Let me give you my number."

"That's not exactly what I said, but, I'll take your number anyway," Tammy said as she smiled and looked up at him.

"It comes with an obligation," said JC taking out his pen.

"What might that be?" she asked.

"If you take it, you must call me within twenty-four hours."

"Twenty-four hours," repeated Tammy.

"Yes, does that seem to be a problem?"

"No, I think I can manage to fulfill that obligation. Oh, and you can call me Tammy."

"I think Tammy is a beautiful name, but not as beautiful as you."

All in one long moment, he looked at the long lashes surrounding her big, beautiful, dark brown eyes that seemed to blink in slow motion. Her very soft high-pitched laughter was unforgettable. His gaze moved from the top of her head downward, following her silky black hair as it fell over her left shoulder and down to where he thought he had better make eye contact again.

Lance noticed the conversation between Tammy and JC and smiled at JC when the two of them made eye contact. If any young man was going to get to know his niece in New York, he was happy for it to be Christopher Jay Michael.

He thought, too, about how well Tory, Arelius and Adreanna were doing since Jake's death. He attributed this both to the fact that their new cousin, Tammy, had come into their lives, and namely towards Eddie, Fran and Karly...these amazing and beautiful encounters of short arisings...

BEYOND ENCOUNTERS

CHAPTER TWENTY-FIVE

Antonio took his noon break away from the hospital. He wanted to talk with his sister about his relationship with Michelle Roby and perhaps get a point or two on the length of relationships and the like. He was glad he had Dez so close now, and could imagine what it would have been like growing up together. The fact that she was ten years older than him made him think how nice it would have been to have had his older sister around when he needed advice

The past is gone, he thought, *and time has vanished for what might have been in having a big sister during elementary and then junior high...besides, by the time I got to high school, she probably would have moved anyway. I'm determined to stay positive about us finally getting back together as a family.*

By the time he arrived at the Feed store for his lunch with Dez, his thoughts had gone full circle.

"Arelius," Dez said as she picked up their sack lunches, "Uncle Antonio and I will be outside at the picnic table if you need me."

"Okay, Mother. Oh, Uncle Antonio, can you give me five minutes before you have to get back to the hospital? I have to tell you the latest about something we had agreed on."

"Sure, Arelius, I'm eager to hear, and I know what you mean," said Antonio, making a thumbs-up signal and clicking his tongue.

Antonio and Dez sat at the shaded picnic table with delightful expressions that showed they were happy to be together, a reunited family. Antonio was anxious to expound further on the conversation they had earlier about Michelle Roby.

"I'm ready, Dez," said Antonio with firm conviction. "I'm ready for a life with Michelle. We've followed the book on proper courtship to the letter. Her mother still has her first good impression of me after all this time. Her brother, Ian, whom you've met, gave me a hard time at first, just to see if I'd stick, I think, but I understand his being protective, and very caring of his only younger sister. He just made me aware of my own feelings in being serious about Michelle. And I *am* serious."

"So, you wanted to talk to me about it, not ask what you should do?" asked Dez.

"Yes. I know what I'm going to do. I'm going to ask her to marry me."

"Are you prepared for rejection to your marriage proposal?"

"I didn't get that far. Should I think along those lines?" asked Antonio, choking a little on the large bite of sandwich.

"If you haven't already, there must be good reason for you not to have thought about that. Do you feel she's ready as well?"

"I do."

Dez laughed. "We're not practicing marriage vows at the moment you know, with that, 'I do'."

"Yeah, I know… kind of sounded like it, huh?"

"For sure it did. But seriously, Antonio," Dez placed her hand on his shoulder, "Since you say you're ready, and I think you are, not that you need my opinion, you know the next step, and the next and the next."

Kiddingly, Antonio said, "It sounds better and better. I think I'll propose tonight."

"Are you serious? Do you have the ring? Did you get it when you went to that doctor's seminar? Did a female help you pick what you think she might like?"

"Slow down, slow down, Sis," said Antonio, holding both hands out as if to say STOP. "Yes, yes, yes, and yes." He reached into his jacket pocket and pulled out a small box. "Here it is. Tell me what you think."

Dez held her breath and opened the case, tears

clouding her vision.

When Antonio saw the tears roll down her cheeks he pulled his handkerchief from his pocket.

"Should I be prepared to produce one of these for Michelle tonight when she sees it?"

"You certainly should be, and make sure it's one of your best ones, like this one," she sobbed as she wrapped her arms around his neck.

"I sure will. Thank you for being here, Dez."

"Thank you for sharing this special occasion with me, Antonio," she said sniffling. "I love you, and I'm so glad we have each other for good times like this and for the unpleasant times that we've had our share of. Oh, and Arelius is so happy you're his uncle and that he can confide in you. I like that, too. Thank you for taking the time with him. I'm aware that you do. Eli and I are both happy about that." She dabbed her eyes once more and handed him the handkerchief.

"No problem, he's a good kid. Well, don't let him hear me call him a 'kid'- he'd be fine about the 'good' part, though. But, he is a good young man. He's going to make a great husband for the right girl."

"Yes, I agree, and I think he wants to do a little 'girl' talk with you. He and Jake used to spend hours on their top bunk beds talking, and I'm sure it wasn't all about the stars they saw." She sighed, "He doesn't talk much about Jake, but I know he misses him very much."

"I know he does. I do too. It doesn't seem real that

he's not with us any more… hmm, it seems the guys over here watch the clock so they can buzz me at least ten minutes before my lunch break is over. I better go see what Arelius wanted to talk about before the buzzer goes off."

"Okay, I'll sit here and finish lunch while the two of you talk," said Dez.

"Sounds like a plan," said Antonio as he kissed her cheek. "I'll let you know how it turns out with Michelle."

"Okay, I'm counting on it."

As he sat down with his nephew, Arelius did not hesitate to get right to the point.

"Uncle Antonio," he began, "once not too long ago you asked me if I had found someone special."

"I remember that conversation, Arelius. Since you're initiating that particular subject, I gather that maybe… just maybe, you have that special one in your life now."

"Yes, I have. I certainly have. Her name is Karly. She lives in New York. I met her one winter when I went to visit Tory and Adreanna. She's the sister of a girl Tory is courting."

"Is it serious?" asked Antonio.

"What? Tory's courting?" Arelius asked in return, in a joking way.

"Well, I do want to know about Tory's courting, but, right now, I had more in mind - you and Karly."

"Oh. Yes, it's serious. She and I have been talking,

writing, and e-mailing each other for over a year now. We keep getting closer and we're thinking seriously about a future together. We're so much alike. She finishes the end of my sentences, like she really listens and understands me. We have a lot of things in common, not only just between the two of us, but also our families. She even writes poems like Mother. It's amazing, Uncle Antonio, how right it feels."

"There's nothing wrong with that kind of thinking, or feeling, for that matter, Arelius, nothing at all. How old are you now anyway?

"I'm twenty-two and will be twenty-three in a few months."

"Well, you're a very serious-minded almost twenty-three year old," said Antonio. "And I'd like to know more as things develop between the two of you. You will keep me updated, won't you?"

"I sure will. So, how are things with you and Michelle Roby? Thought you were going to escape that question from me, huh?"

"That thought did cross my mind."

Just as Antonio was about to fill Arelius in on the latest news about his relationship with Michele, his pager went off. As he glanced down at it, Arelius said the old cliché, "*Saved by the bell,*" and laughed.

"Yes, you're right. To be continued, and I look forward to taking up where we've left off. There's something I needed to talk with you about, now that you asked about Michelle and me."

His curiosity piqued, Arelius asked, "I detect something serious in your tone. When would you like for us to get together?"

"Let's do breakfast at the Internet Café in the morning. Is that good for you?"

"Sure."

"How about an early one, say about seven? And it's on me."

"I always knew we were on the same wavelength. That'll make it an even better breakfast. See you then."

Smiling, Antonio said, "You'll have your share of tabs to pick up when you take Karly out. So it's the least I can do. Hey, fill me in on how Tory and Adreanna are doing in New York over breakfast."

"Alright, I'll be glad to catch you up to speed."

"Good, I'm going now. See you."

BEYOND ENCOUNTERS

CHAPTER TWENTY-SIX

It's so very interesting, Brant thought to himself, as once again he sat alone on his front porch swing, *how time brings about a change in our lives. The things that take place within our lives are first and foremost governed by time and unforeseen circumstances.* Tonight, while on his porch waiting for the lights to go out at his daughter's house, he thought about his grandchildren. He lingered in his thoughts about how thankful he was that Arelius visited regularly and what a great help he was around the property.

Brant remembered once when Arelius, after helping out at the feed store, arrived at his place hoping to operate the tractor that was used to unload hay. On this particular visit, Arelius asked him, "Grandfather, there's this idea I'm going to ask you about, well, I know it would take business away from our feed store if you actually did it, but, why is it that you don't use a portion of your property for bailing hay?"

"You know, Arelius, that thought has crossed my mind more than a few times. I think about it when we go to your dad's feed store. That would be a monumental task. I mean planting, irrigating, cutting and bailing; I would have to have someone with a strong back to do all of it. If I could find the right man for the job, I would want to do that very much. I don't want to engage your uncle Arthur for that job. He helps out here so much already. And now, with the sudden death of their daughter, Penny, well, I just don't want to put too much on him, although, I have a feeling that if I decided to do what you're asking about, he would take it on as a project he felt he had to do."

"It may be just what Uncle Arthur needs, Grandfather." Arelius was balancing on the edge of one of the steps and seemed to be losing interest in anything outside of the challenge of making it to the other side. "Well, if you ever decide, just remember, I'll be glad to help. I have no plans to go too far from Hallettsville."

"Okay, Arelius, I'll remember that. I always thought you'd stay close to home. So how will that sit with the prospective bride when she comes along?"

"Not you, *too,* Grandfather!" He could feel the

embarrassment that he was certain showed on his face. "You sound like Uncle Antonio. He never manages to have a conversation with me without bringing up the subject of *her,*" he said. As he finished brushing the grass off of his jeans, he stood tall and motioned quotation marks when he said *her.*

"Sounds like Antonio may have ideas of his own about a *"her"* for himself," said grandfather with a smile, trying hard not to laugh at Arelius' acrobatics.

"You're right on the money, Grandfather. Something is up with him, but I don't know the details yet. He assured me he would let me know if and when." By this time, he was seated next to Brant in the swing, legs dangling loose over the edge as he tried to reach the porch with his toes.

"Well, it's about time! I won't say anything to him about any of this talk of ours," Brant assured his grandson, patting him on the back.

"Okay, and I'll keep you posted. I think he wants to be absolutely certain before he talks with you about things."

"I'm sure you're right. And you will let me know when your girl comes along?"

"Yes sir, I will," said Arelius nodding, hoping his grandfather could not see his embarrassment reappearing.

"Oh, by the way, Arelius," Brant continued, "Where would you live when you settle down with your bride?"

"Here, Grandfather, why?"

"I'll bet I could just about guess where you'd want your house."

"Think you could? Okay where?" He jumped off the porch swing, faced his grandfather with arms across his chest and feet wide apart.

"I think you'd like a log cabin in the Branch, probably near that stream down there. Am I close?"

Arelius was always amazed at how his grandfather knew things. He just shook his head. "Once again, you're right on the money."

"Well, when you're ready for your log cabin, just let me know... I want it to be an early wedding gift."

Arelius opened his eyes wide in disbelief. "Really? Are you sure, Grandfather?"

"I'm as sure as we're having this conversation! Do we have a deal?" He reached out in an invitation to shake hands.

Arelius nodded his head vigorously, and his handshake was equally as vigorous. "Yes sir! We sure do!"

After recalling the conversation he had with Arelius, and while still sitting on his porch, Brant thought about what a good relationship he and Suzanna had with Eli and the good relationship he knew his daughter had with her mother-in-law, Alice.

Eli had always gotten along with Dez's mother as

if she were his own. Suzanna thought highly of Eli and treated him like a son. Eli and Brant had gotten along ever since he found out Brant's identity.

Both Eli and Dez would never in any way, fashion, or form, go along with the so-called, mother-in-law jokes or any kind of jokes that cast a bad light on the relationship the two of them had with each other's parents, and would shield that beautiful relationship from such misinformed attackers.

Dez and Eli agreed that Dez had the characteristics of Eli's mother, Alice, and that she could be her daughter with no problem. At times when Dez did manifest Alice's feisty characteristics, Eli would refer to Dez as *Ms. Alice*. Dez had no choice but to agree. Further, Eli called Dez *Ms.* Ruby. Ruby was Alice's mother. She lived in San Angelo, Texas. At age ninety-three, and all of four foot two, she lived alone and was very independent. She also had a feisty disposition, and if called upon to do so, would easily be able to hold a conversation with the President of the United States on any given topic.

Occasionally Dez visited Ruby. On a recent visit, Dez jotted down a conversation she and Ruby had that made her chuckle.

Ruby told Dez about the time she had gone to the Concho River to fish. There, next to her, lay her pistol.

Ruby said to Dez. "Along came the game warden. He asked me if I was catching anything. I told him, yeah, snakes and turtles. Then he said, "Ms. Ruby, didn't you see that sign that said 'no firearms are allowed on the river'?"

Ruby's first response to Dez was that she told the game warden she did not see it. The second time Ruby told Dez that same story she said she told the game warden that she forgot that there was a sign that prohibited firearms. Dez thought that if Ruby told the story a third time, she would change it again.

Dez could not stay for such storytelling because she had to get back home. Her daughter-in-law, Karly, had begun labor, and her OBGYN doctor, Dr. Alex Glendale, was taking no chances with the unexpected timetable the baby himself had set.

While driving back to Hallettsville from San Angelo, Dez reflected on the nice memories she had of times with her mother, and thought of how alone her father was without Suzanna LeAnn. Before she left for San Angelo, she had come across an online cake service. When she read what appeared to be a motto on the website, it brought tears to her eyes. It read, "If you miss the delicious cakes your sweet mother used to bake, you've come to the right place." It touched Dez so much that the first butter pound cake she ordered she only ordered out of a need to feel close to her mother again. After tasting the cake and after she shared it with her father, they agreed that not only was it similar to the cakes Suzanna used to bake; they were indeed as delicious as the ad had claimed.

There came a time when no cakes were available. But to their delight, Michelle Roby's mother, after recuperating from her broken hip, began making lemon butter pound cakes that equaled Suzanna's.

Brant became the best of friends with Ina Roby due to the fact that their children, Michelle and Antonio saw a future together and it made Brant and Ina very happy.

Now, as the lights in the house across the pasture began one by one to disappear into the blackness of the night, he thought about his grandchildren and how things had turned out for them. Tory and Fran saw each other beyond their first encounter, and after a long courtship they were married on May 27, 2000, in Bronx, New York. Eli delivered the marriage talk. During the reception, Tory surprised Fran with a touching musical skit based on a song with words that reflected how he felt that she had been towards him since their first encounter. Her love, her strength, and all the times she stood by him were highlights of the song. He had rehearsed the skit with a few of his friends and it went very well. Eddie proposed to Adreanna in London just past midnight on

January 1, 2003. They were married August 14, 2003, on the island of St. Lucia. It was a wedding on the beach and everything took place just as she had visualized when younger. Also, Adreanna was so happy when her life-long dream of her very own art exhibit at New York's SoHo Gallery, owned by Eddie's sister, Olivia, became a reality. Arelius was at the country house and worked at the feed store, as well as helped out his grandfather. He began courting Karly and during the courtship, Arelius made numerous trips to New York to visit her. The last trip he made, he proposed. Beforehand, Arelius had spoken with Karly's parents and informed them that he was going to propose to their daughter on his next trip to New York. They appreciated Arelius' old-fashioned way of asking for their consent and gave their approval. In preparation for the proposal, Arelius bought the engagement ring and asked for a 'cute' box that he could use as a plan. He told the sales clerk about his idea and so took the bread tie he had taken from home and placed it in a pink sparkling ring box. On August 20, 2004, he, Karly and her friend, Aleisha, went to dinner to Olive Garden at Times Square. After dinner, Arelius got out of his chair and went over to Karly. He turned her around to face him while she was still seated. He got down on one knee and asked her if she would marry him. He held her hands as the box was there on the table. She did not see it because as she cried, her focus was only on Arelius' face. Her friend had to say, "Karly, look at the table already." Karly looked and only then did she see the box. She opened it and saw the bread tie. She smiled and was convinced more than ever that he was indeed a unique guy. She said, yes, and immediately Arelius placed the 'true' engagement ring on her finger. Afterwards, they went dancing and then he took Karly and her friend home. Arelius and Karly married on January 8, 2005, in Texas City, Texas, where her parents had moved.

Now, with his mind full and satisfied, Brant sighed deeply as he motioned a kiss with his hand outstretched toward his daughter's home and slowly shuffled into the house, retiring to bed at the end of another beautiful day.

BEYOND ENCOUNTERS

CHAPTER TWENTY-SEVEN

In preparation for her writing on Cape Cod, Eli, Tory and Fran planned to take Dez on a short trip of discovery. They wanted to explore the area and find the best place for her to be alone to finish the part of her novel that she was determined to get down on paper. Before that trip she needed to talk with Antonio.

They engaged in lengthy conversation wherein she expressed her admiration for his having stood in for his colleague at the doctor's seminar in Connecticut. Antonio filled her in on his experience there:

While at the Medical Convention, lo and behold, he met someone who had taken a temporary OBGYN position in their neighboring city of Victoria. He told Dez that the name of the doctor was Alex Glendale. Dr. Glendale's display was adjacent to his.

What caught Antonio's attention about Dr. Glendale, and what lead to their short encounter, was the conversation he overheard the group having when someone mentioned the name of a hospital near Hallettsville, Texas. After Antonio took the position at Yoakum's Hospital, he received offers to join the medical staff at the very hospital he overheard the group of OBGYN doctors talking about, namely, the DeNor Hospital.

Dr. Glendale noticed his raised eyebrows. He spoke across the table. "I couldn't help but overhear the name DeNor, the name of a hospital I declined an offer to practice medicine there several years ago. Does one of the doctors in your group practice there?" He caught himself, "Oh, how rude of me. I'm Antonio Chamberlain, attending in the place of one of the doctors from the Yoakum Hospital."

"That's quite alright. I'm Alex Glendale. And DeNor was to be my permanent destination right after med school, but I took a detour for a few years. The hospital could use several more OBGYN doctors."

"I see," Antonio interjected. "And you're thinking of staying there?"

"I *have* been giving it serious thought, yes. I'm not too sure if I could get used to a city with less than one million people. What has me considering being permanent at DeNor is that it's one of the best facilities."

Antonio realized that he had dominated the conversation, with the recounting of his encounter with Dr. Glendale, for the past several minutes and after apologizing, expressed his appreciation to Dez for her attentiveness and also over the fact that she had made a special trip to see him before she left for the Cape.

It did not cross her mind to do anything other than to have stayed and listened to her brother talk, she would have stayed even longer. She missed not growing up together. Before departing, Dez asked Antonio to look after Arelius and their father while she was away and told him not to hesitate to call her if Brant got sick and needed her.

They hugged and parted company.

Before making firm plans for Cape Cod, Dez rang a place called Onset Village Inn and spoke to the owner, Jeanette. She told her that she was in search of a place conducive for writing, as she was finishing a novel. The pictures and description of the Inn that Dez found on the internet seemed to Dez to be the perfect place.

Jeanette assured Dez that her place would inspire her and that it had a picture window that faced the Bay. She felt that Dez would love it there.

Shortly after arriving in Cape Cod, the family enjoyed a very friendly welcome from the manager of the Onset Village Inn. He showed them around and showed them the studio apartment Dez would probably stay in when she returned. It was exactly what she expected, and they all liked it very much.

They thanked him for his time and explained there were a few more properties they wanted to see. He graciously walked them out and sent them on their way.

They looked at several other places but everyone agreed that the Onset Village Inn was the place for Mother to stay. They knew that, since it was a small village, Dez would enjoy walking here and there. Dez had noticed an eye-catching lighthouse visible from the Inn and although she did not know exactly how, she knew that this lighthouse would somehow hold fond memories for her.

As they all traveled back to New York where Tory and Fran lived, the lighthouse stood out vividly in her mind. She rested her head on Eli's shoulder and reflected on her future stay at the Inn.

She and Eli had a plan. They would travel to the Cape together. Eli would make sure she was ready for her long stay and, after a few days, he would leave her there, but not for long.

Early in their marriage, they had agreed *"We won't be apart from each other on regular extended leaves, no matter what."* With raising the family and all of the extended-family emergencies, they were determined not to forget their agreement.

After leaving Tory and Fran in New York, Dez and Eli went home, happy in their decision to use Onset Village Inn on her return trip. They planned for Dez to stay there in late Fall. In the months between their return and her eventual writing vacation, they were blessed with their first grandchild, Micah Eli Ortello. Arelius and Karly had planned to have children soon after they were married. True to Arelius' promise to be the first to have children, the first to provide his parents with grandchildren, little Micah arrived as planned. Dez's heart glowed when she thought about Brant being able to enjoy his first great grandbaby.

Autumn arrived quickly and since family and business matters were in good order, Eli and Dez set out for Onset Village.

Arriving late on Sunday, they decided to wait until the morning to look at their surroundings. Before turning in for the night, they talked about their first encounter at the University of Hallettsville. They spent hours recalling many things that happened beyond their first encounter, things that had a direct bearing on where they found themselves right then.

Morning's presence once again showed itself to be reliable and dependable. Eli had set the small-faced alarm clock so that they could wake up early enough to witness the beautiful, perfect and powerful display of the rising sun.

After experiencing the early morning sunrise, they walked quietly hand in hand down the shoreline, listening to the quiet water lapping against the shore as the boats passed in the distance. Eli knew he would leave the next morning for his early flight home. Standing on the shoreline with Dez's face in his big strong hands, Eli said, "Two weeks, Dez, and I'll be back. Will you be okay my lil' Red Riding Hood?"

"Knowing that you will return soon, I will be. I'll write non-stop until I see you again."

Before saying his next words, he tenderly kissed her, a kiss that reminded her of the goodnight kiss, the one he gave her the night he proposed to her, after which she wrote the poem *Goodnight Kiss*. He then said, "Dez, my dear sweet, Dez. Time will fly by and we'll be together again. The next sunrise we'll see together, although you'll be here and I'll be back in Texas. No, I'll be on the plane, a little closer to it than you. It doesn't matter, we'll be together to enjoy another sunrise that'll come through that bay window up there," he said as he pointed in the direction of the studio apartment. "It will invite itself gradually into our room and then shine on our faces to uncover the joy we have at being together."

"Eli, I tell you the truth, I really do love you."

"I love you too, Dez."

A small sailboat passed in the distance making them aware that they were not alone. With that interruption, Eli continued, "I've been known to get hungry every morning. How about we go to that restaurant over there? What is the name of it?"

Before Dez could respond, he said excitedly, "Oh there, I see it! It's called Pier View. Hungry?"

231

"Yes, I am. That's a great idea, but I have to warn you, I have a gigantic appetite. It'll be a going away breakfast, and when the time comes for me to leave, we'll do a going away breakfast for the both of us because we'll be going home together."

"That sounds good to me. But did I detect what I thought I detected?" asked Eli as his dimpled smile surfaced.

"Whatever do you mean?" Dez asked with a smirk.

In the past, whenever Dez used the phrase, "but I'll have to warn you", it was followed by some good-humored maneuver.

Eli continued. "Because I detected that if we were back at the apartment, there would have been cause for a pillow fight after that warning. It would be one we'd do alone, without the children barreling into our room to join in the fun. It would be pretty interesting to see what the outcome of a pillow fight on Cape Cod would be." As Eli spoke he moved away from Dez anticipating some unknown tease.

"Why a pillow fight?" She caught Eli off guard, wrapping her right leg behind his right knee while at the same time grabbing his shoulders, and she dropped him to the sand. It was a maneuver she learned while in junior high school. While Eli was on the ground, she ran off to the nearby restaurant and waited for him on the steps.

Eli was so shocked that he had been caught off guard that he stayed there looking up at the sky as if he were not going to join Dez at the Pier View Restaurant.

"Come on!" shouted Dez, "the coffee is getting cold!"

Eli, completely embarrassed, slowly got up and smiled all the way to her. He said, "And I thought I was *your* bodyguard. I think you'll be able to handle yourself just fine when I leave, yep, just fine." He put his arm around her and they entered the restaurant.

BEYOND ENCOUNTERS

CHAPTER TWENTY-EIGHT

Dez was up bright and early. She wanted to keep the same walk routine she and Eli started while he was with her. Her walk began right at the street outside her studio apartment. A cobblestone sidewalk followed the line of the street which followed the curvature of the shoreline a short distance past the lawn on the other side. The elevation gave the illusion that the water began right at the crest of the hill which began to descend a short distance from the street. As she walked toward the village the sidewalk began to divert away from following the flow of the beach and took on its own path, leading her to the park, on past the gazebo, and finally into the hub of the village with its gift shops, little restaurants and bookstores, now quiet compared to the hustle of peak season activity.

One shop in particular was the local book store. Dez recalled when she and Eli stopped in and got a feel from the owner of what people in the area were interested in. The owner, Mali, was very helpful and happy that Dez was going to be a local for the month. She preordered several copies of the novel and placed a copy in the display window next to several best seller novels. This added to the inspiration Dez already felt.

When she and Eli left the bookstore, Eli took her hand and fervently said, "Just follow me, Dez, and I'll take you places. See what just happened? You're going to be considered a local author right here in Onset Village, and people will pass this window and see your first novel."

Her exact response was, "Oh, Eli, I'm so excited! No, thrilled! No, I'm ecstatic!"

She could not help but recall her time with Eli as she walked through Onset Village and adamantly disapproved of the saying, "Out of sight out of mind." It was certainly *not* the case with Eli having gone back to Texas. He would be on her mind at all times and she had no doubt that it was the same for him.

Dez's brisk walk ended at the Pier View Restaurant situated directly on a corner. The view of the pier from the restaurant beckoned passersby to come in and enjoy a perfect breakfast. The restaurant was not crowded. There were four people sitting at a table next to a window across from Dez, where she, too, had chosen a window view. *No doubt seeing the pier contributed to the name of the restaurant,* Dez thought. She was so engrossed in the view and her own thoughts that she barely heard the waitress ask for the third time, "Coffee, ma'am?"

Her stern tone of voice jolted Dez out of her thoughts.

"Oh, yes, please," Dez said apologetically.

At that point, a voice from the table near Dez whispered, "Don't be so nice to her, you make me look like a meanie."

Dez smiled and under her breath playfully said in a deep voice, "Hurry with that cup of coffee, will ya?"

Both the lady at that table and the rest of the folks with her laughed, and the lady said, "Now you're talking."

Dez smiled as the waitress approached her table. She served the coffee and Dez said very quietly, yet happily, "Thank you very much."

In response to all the *thank you's* that would follow from Dez, the waitress said *you're welcome* each time.

When Dez went to the register to pay her bill, she and the waitress got into a conversation about why Dez was at Onset Village. She told Dez her name was Alice. The mention of the name Alice immediately brought forth an enthusiastic response from Dez. "Alice is a character in the novel I'm finishing up here! In fact, she's one of the main characters."

The waitress said, "Then your novel will do well since my name is in it."

That remark brought a smile to Dez with many memories of her mother-in-law, Alice, particularly the ones when she frequented the back room of their country home.

She acknowledged the waitress' comment and left to complete her morning walk.

Dez knew the time was approaching that would mark the end of the writing project she had begun a year ago. She had purposely allowed distraction after distraction to interrupt the finishing of the book. She felt as if it would close a chapter in her life, a chapter she did not want to end. She came to tears many times as she contemplated the journey she knew she had to undertake to complete the task ahead of her. It would require intense feelings surrounding the death of her second son, Jake. Just as his life had started and progressed as he grew to a young man and then was no more, so her writing had started and progressed, and it, too, would come to an end. How angry with man's greatest enemy she was. *Death*, she thought, *was truly the greatest, most cruel enemy one could ever know.*

Her only consolation, if one could exist, was the fact that Jake had accomplished many things he had hoped to do. She knew this after she and Eli found a list while clearing out his apartment in Eagle Pass, Texas. He had written and checked off a list of short-term goals he wanted very much to accomplish and did, all of which had to do with helping people. Dez would always remember his most giving and joyful spirit, to which anyone who met him, would attest. At the bottom of the list he had written one long-term goal, *get married to Rachel.* That goal never became a reality.

The biggest distraction to Dez came one night when a frightful brawl broke out near her apartment and ended up at her front door. She heard angry voices as the dispute escalated and moved closer and closer. At her front door the two men fought in such a way that the outer glass storm door was broken. Dez saw the man's bloody shirt through the French doors, surely to be the next broken. She became frightened and called 911, which brought police cars and an ambulance, flooding her apartment with flashing red, blue and blinding white lights. Passersby stood in disbelief at what they witnessed in the normally quiet community.

After the disturbance was over, she talked with Eli for about an hour and a half and felt better about staying in the studio for the remainder of her stay at Onset Village.

She was glad to see morning. It came with no visible sun, only cloudiness over the bay and thick fog hovering over it and her immediate area. The fog lifted gradually. There was a scene that began to appear very close to Dez's studio apartment. The news of the feud the night before was spreading. She observed one person and then another and another gather on the porch of the Victorian Inn next door.

Dez observed the official greeter on the porch. Whether appointed or whether self-designated, he embraced each person as they went up the steps and onto the porch to talk about the previous night's excitement. The manager of the Inn made an appearance at the front porch of the Inn each time someone passed the breezeway that separated Dez's studio apartment from the Inn. His living quarters were located at the back of the property.

The greeter, with his short beard and smiling face, seemed to re-enact the brawl with new arrivals. Each time he pointed in Dez's direction, no doubt pointing out that her glass door was missing because of having been smashed in during the fight.

Eli informed Brant about the brawl. Right away Brant called Lance in New York. He told him about the terrible incident. Before Brant was able to suggest what he thought would be an imposition, Lance said, "You know, Brant, I've always wanted to go to Cape Cod. I think this would be as good a time as any, that is, if you don't mind. But if you'd rather go and check on your daughter yourself, I'll understand."

"Lance, I haven't been feeling well for the past few months. I haven't told Dez - or Eli for that matter. I wanted her to go finish her book... it's so important to her. Had she known I wasn't well, she would be here right now. When she told me that she was going away to finish her novel, she was filled with enthusiasm. I just couldn't dampen her spirits and risk her not being there this very moment. I feel bad that this incident happened right at her apartment door. Lance, I'd be grateful if you would go see her."

"No more need to be said, my brother."

Brant recalled another time when he needed Lance. It was the time young Lance had come to his rescue when they were living at home in Paris. Lance ran as fast as he could to tell Arthur about the bully who was picking on him. He remembered telling Lance that he would never forget what he had done in telling Arthur about that bully and if the time ever came when trouble found him, he knew he would be there for him. He looked at Lance's going to Cape Cod to check on Dez as such a time.

"I'd be more than happy to go," Lance continued. "And after I've seen her, I'll inform you right away."

"Thank you, Lance, thank you so very much. After all these years you're still right there for me when I need you. I'm certainly glad I didn't get the classic black eye after a hit from that bully, and no doubt it would have been *me* falling into that mud puddle instead of him, had it not been for you and Arthur."

They both had a laugh about yesteryear, after which Lance said, "You're welcome. Take care of yourself, Brant."

"I will, and you, too. Be safe in your traveling, and please let Dez know I'm thinking of her and also that I'm doing okay for an old guy. Oh, and Lance, will you let her know that I'm enjoying the lemon butter pound cake she ordered online for me from Ina before she left for Cape Cod? "

"I most certainly will pass on all of your words to her, Brant."

BEYOND ENCOUNTERS

CHAPTER TWENTY-NINE

When he arrived in Onset Village, Lance checked into the Harbor Watch Inn, which was owned by Meg Kistin. The Inn had three floors that accommodated its guests, and was one of the beautiful Victorian styled Inns in the area. Located in the same block as the Inn on Onset Bay where Dez was staying, Lance secured room 2B on the second floor. It had a balcony that provided a most spectacular view overlooking the bay.

After he checked in and met Meg Kistin and her assistant, Linda, Lance was off up the cobblestone sidewalk to see Dez.

With a large smile and a screech of joy she hugged her uncle and kissed him on his right cheek. After exchanging brief family pleasantries, they sat at the table by the picture window and Dez gave Lance an assessment of what had happened on the night of the brawl. Lance was comforted as she assured him that she was doing well and everything was now fine. She told him that the Innkeeper, Joe, and his wife, Susie, were at her doorstep immediately and that they committed to be there for her if she needed anything because everything had been taken care of regarding the brawl.

"That reassurance," said Dez softly, "has been wonderfully calming for me, so I'm doing okay and I'm determined to stay here in Onset Village, in *my* studio apartment to finish what I came here to do."

"Oh my, it's *her* studio apartment she says," Lance mocked sarcastically, teasing her.

"Yes, yes it is," said Dez in a matter-of-fact way. "And before I leave, I'm going to reserve it for next year, for about this same time, except that next time, Eli will be with me for the whole month."

He stood up to view the bay from different angles as he walked around the small room, finally stopping at the door, folding his hands behind him as he rocked on his heels.

"That sounds very romantic, Dez. I admire the close relationship you and Eli have. Valtora and I have a good marital example to look at in the marriage you and Eli have."

"Well thank you, Uncle Lance."

"You're quite welcome." He returned to the table

and sat down. "And before I forget, young lady, your father asked me to let you know that he's thinking of you and that he's doing okay 'for an old guy'."

He could not hold his chuckle in, "And he wanted me to let you know that he received the lemon butter pound cake that you ordered for him before you left." He turned and peered at Dez with a mock-frown. "Am I missing out on something? What's with this ordering cake, online is it?"

"First, thank you for delivering that long list of messages from Dad. I've been a little worried about him lately. I don't think he's aware of my concern. I can't wait to get back home to him. Second, about ordering cakes, and yes, online, well, I've been doing that for him for some time now. The reason I began ordering them was because of what the lady had written on her website."

"What in the world was written on her website?"

"It read, *'If you miss the delicious cakes your sweet mother used to bake, you've come to the right place.'* Uncle Lance, that touched me so much, I cried after reading it. I think what I read compelled me to order the first one, and then after tasting it, I ordered another, and then for one Dad, and then one for Eli. She had all kinds of butter pound cake flavors. I think I've about ordered them all, but my favorite is the same as Dad's: lemon. Suddenly, they were no longer available. But then, to our surprise, Mr. Ian Roby's mother, Ina Roby, began baking and selling them online. They were just as delicious as the ones we had ordered in the past."

"Ahhh. Ian's mother. Well, I had no idea she made cakes.

Sounds like you guys have the best kept secret. I'll have to get her website address from you and perhaps Ina Roby and I can do business for my restaurant with her cakes."

"That sounds like a nice thing to do, Uncle Lance." Dez was thrilled at the prospect.

"All this talk of cake – let's go to dinner. Hungry?" asked Lance as he stood up and offered his arm.

She put her arm through his as she stood up. "Yes, I am. But I miss Eli more than I'm hungry."

"You'll be with Eli soon. But, you have to eat to stay healthy in the meantime."

"You're right. What's your pleasure? I'm game for whatever you'd like."

Kidding, Lance said, "Well, what I'd really like is a Texas size chicken fried steak. But since we're in seafood territory, let's do lobster."

"Okay, and since you said I have to eat an' all, can we make that *steak* and lobster?"

"Absolutely."

"Oh, Uncle Lance, when I ordered that cake from Ina Roby for Dad, I also ordered one for me and had it delivered here. So you'll get a chance to try her lemon butter pound cake after dinner."

"I'll look forward to that, Dez."

They enjoyed a wonderful meal together, and afterwards Dez noticed that Lance signed the credit card receipt, 'Lance R. Haggerty'.

"What does that 'R' stand for - Roger?"

"Exactly! Wow! What a guess!" he exclaimed.

"I had no idea, honest. You kind of remind me of a Roger."

"Oh, I do, do I?"

"Yes, you do. It's so nice having you here even though you will be leaving in a few days. Since you're here I feel secure. You've made me forget about that fight and my bashed in glass door. Your presence did contribute to how I'm feeling now, but what *I* think did it was that gift you brought me, all wrapped up. You still haven't told me how you knew that was my favorite candy."

"Well, when I want to know a certain thing I have my ways, and I won't disclose my secret source."

"Okay, I won't pry, but I do know that I'll never be able finish off the whole box of Whatchamacallits. It's my favorite candy for sure, but a *whole box* of them! Uncle Lance Roger Haggerty, you really wanted my mind off of that brawl."

"Yes, that was the intended goal, Dez, but evidently you didn't find the true surprise in the box."

Needless to say, they were out of the restaurant and back at her studio in no time. She emptied the entire box of candy on to the table at the bay window. There among the candy bars she saw…*nothing*.

"I don't see anything," said Dez.

"Well, if you would just turn around for a second you just may see your real surprise."

She turned in the direction of her small kitchen and there stood Eli, smiling widely producing his embedded left cheek dimple. Dez screamed his name and her excitement was evident. She turned and hugged her uncle and then ran to Eli's waiting arms. Eli ran his hands through her hair and said, "Don't be afraid, my lil' Red Riding Hood." He kissed her forehead and then laid his right cheek on that kiss. They never noticed Uncle Lance leave the apartment to retire in his room at the Harbor Watch Inn.

This encounter that Lance arranged was sure to accomplish what he had intended... for Dez to forget that upsetting night of the brawl when the glass door went falling onto the steps just outside her studio apartment.

Although Eli and Dez had only said goodbye less than a week before, to them it felt as if they had been apart the whole month.

With the unexpected pleasure of Eli's visit, the remaining time would fly by and soon Dez would be home, the two of them would lie down in their own bed and awaken to the morning sunrise lying next to each other as had always been the case. The completion of her writing about Jake's death would be the beginning of their life together without him, something that to the present the two of them were still trying to cope with.

Life goes on despite tragedy, it was the subject the two of them discussed at length, but now with a deeper appreciation for the richness of life, for people, for breathing, touching, hearing, smelling, and seeing.

They spoke of how awesome it was to see the beautiful, most grand creation all around, hearing its sounds, sensing touch and experiencing its taste. Nothing was lacking, *nothing at all* they would say.

Once again, Eli left but not before building up Dez's confidence and giving her the support she needed, assuring her that all would work out while she finished her intended purpose of being in Cape Cod. With Uncle Lance around for the next few days, Dez would concentrate on finishing her novel, so that when Eli did come for her, the book on that part of their life would be finished.

Lance wined and dined Dez at the Harbor Watch Inn's most elegant restaurant, with white table cloths and candles on every table. "What memories, Uncle Lance, thank you for them," Dez would say after each outing with him before he left.

But now that both Eli and her uncle were gone, she felt much better about what had transpired with the fight, and Dez focused on her writing. She took time to sit on the marbled bench across the street. Inscribed on its back were the words, "Take time to sit by the Sea." It was a bench she sat on many times while she meditated on her life… her life with Eli, her family, and especially with Jake. Tears clouded the figures of the sea gulls passing overhead as their piercing sound brought her out of her meditation. She smiled, cried, and laughed all in one sitting, after which she felt compelled to go to her studio and write and write and write.

She wrote until she saw morning.

It was no cloudy morning this morning. She was greeted with a beautiful display of the sunrise's most awesome, perfect orange roundness, and she smiled with renewed vigor which lasted only as long as a blossoming delicate flower that withers from the sun's heat. She was so exhausted that she went over to the bed and slept until the moon showed itself.

The next morning Dez felt much better, and later than normal, she went for a walk. It was a bit early for lunch, but she had skipped breakfast and Uncle Lance Roger Haggerty's voice about staying healthy rang in her ears. She thought she would try Marc Anthony's Pizzeria. On its menu's front cover, it boasted of having the "Biggest Menu on Cape Cod." That along with "WE DELIVER" boldly on the front cover was a plus to Dez.

Upon entering Marc Anthony's, Dez picked up a menu at the cashier's station as directed by the large sign located well above the cash register. A man was at the register and Dez asked, "Excuse me, who is Marc Anthony?"

The man said, "I am."

Surprised, Dez said, "Oh! Hi, my name is Dez."

In an effort to support the fact that he indeed was Marc Anthony, he took his wallet out and produced evidence after evidence that he was Marc Anthony. It seemed a bit funny to Dez to observe the entire photo authentication before her, because each photograph was indeed Marc Anthony, although with different hairstyles, different smiles, different poses, etc. She was convinced it was him.

While waiting for her order, Dez sat in the perfect location, right by the window to view people walking through the village and that one squirrel that seemed to follow her no matter where she went. It amused her when she heard Marc Anthony's voice ascend above the chatter of the customers, whether taking orders over the telephone in his humorous way or just talking about one thing or another. He had a friendly way and was comedian-like to his customers.

Before leaving, Dez informed Marc Anthony that she would return to his restaurant because she liked the food and because his restaurant was very interesting. Dez had not been able to look at all of the memorabilia on the walls and throughout the restaurant, not to mention the collage of pictures located down a hallway that lead to the cleanest restroom she had ever come across, with the exception on her own bathroom at the Inn.

Saturday found Dez at Marc Anthony's again. With this visit she hoped to get his permission to use his name and the name of his restaurant as a non-fiction part of her novel. When she entered the restaurant, now experienced with the procedure, she obtained a menu and went to her favorite table. A young man was sitting at the table directly in front of Dez. All would have remained comfortable for Dez had he not turned and stared at her face to face. She recognized him from the day before when she was sitting on the bench overlooking the bay. He watched her there, too, which made her feel uncomfortable, so she got up and went back to the apartment. She noticed he immediately moved to her bench as soon as she was gone.

Dez thought it would be a good idea to ask the young girl at the cash register if the young man was okay. She left her blue jean jacket on the table and went to the young girl and said, "Excuse me, is that young man over there at that table..."

Dez turned to make a subtle indication to where he was, and to her surprise, he had moved her jacket to where he was sitting, and had taken her shaded table!

When the young girl saw to whom Dez was referring, she said, "Oh he's handicapped. He comes in here all the time. You can sit somewhere else in here, I won't ask him to move."

Dez thought to herself only for a second and then said, "Oh no, I was just wanting to know if he was okay. Thank you. I prefer the window where I am, well, was. But he can have my table. Oh, is Marc Anthony here?"

"No, my father will be in later this evening."

"Okay, when he gets here, I'd like to speak with him," Dez said in the same straightforward tone.

When Dez got back to her table, she knew that she did not want to leave the restaurant before the young girl heard what she had to say about the way she handled the situation with the young man.

Dez sat where the young man had placed her jacket at *his* table, but the sun was a bit much, so Dez moved to another shaded table. Had it not been for the view that Marc Anthony so privileged his customers with from all locations in his restaurant, Dez's thought was to take her meal to the gazebo that overlooked the bay where she and Eli had made memories with snuggles and high school behavior.

Marc Anthony arrived very shortly after Dez sat down. Dez approached him and said, "Excuse me, Marc Anthony, may I speak with you?"

In his pronounced voice he said, "Sure, what is it that I can help you with?" He asked this question almost without turning around, which was no surprise to Dez, but the onlookers were waiting, as was his daughter, to hear Dez's next words.

"I was hoping to get your permission to use your

name, and the name of your restaurant in my novel. May I?"

Marc Anthony turned and looked at Dez and said, "You look like you have a good face. Sure, just don't say anything bad about me."

Dez smiled and assured him by saying, "I won't write anything bad about you, it'll be all good. And thanks."

Marc Anthony introduced Dez to his daughter, Ashley, his son Alex, and said, "There's a Jr. around here somewhere."

Dez was ready to leave, but first had a few words for Ashley, his beautiful and spunky daughter.

"When you have a minute, Ashley, I'd like to speak with you."

She said okay and as soon as the register was clear, she went over to Dez.

"Ashley," began Dez, leaning forward so everyone in the restaurant would not hear what she was about to say. In sincerity Dez continued, "I just wanted you to know that I appreciate the protective way you had in regard to that young handicapped boy. The way you told me about not asking him to move, but, that I could move instead, well, it was so impressed on my mind I just couldn't leave without commending you about your care of him. I loved it. I also wanted you to know that I'll write it into my novel just exactly how you said it."

Dez felt that Ashley's response was genuine.

They both smiled and Dez left, knowing that the next time she and Ashley would meet in her father's restaurant, or anywhere in Onset Village for that matter, they would meet as friends because of that young boy who reminded Dez of Jake and his handicap, a word Ashley used, and that Dez was all too familiar with. In the days ahead Dez did go into Marc Anthony's Pizzeria and a smile from Ashley was touching to her. She knew she would always remember her encounter with the wonderful family of Marc Anthony.

BEYOND ENCOUNTERS

CHAPTER THIRTY

Again Dez went for a walk in the crispness of the morning's awakening call. She soon found that her mind was going faster than her stride, so she dashed into the local grocery store and bought a five-theme notebook and a pen to capture thoughts that were quickly filling her mind, and that now, with pen in hand, so fluidly emptied onto the paper.

She was at the gazebo situated on top of the hill in the small park that overlooked the bay where she and Eli had sat the day before, where they not only took in their beautiful surroundings with plentiful trees, but also where they took pictures of each other.

When Dez finally looked up from writing down all her thoughts she observed an absolutely beautiful day...

white clouds hanging in the light blue sky, as if someone, *no not just someone,* she thought, *but an expert painter,* had painted them with the utmost care.

And there, on the bay, in the not so far distance, she saw a live picture-postcard view of different kinds and sizes of boats, from the kayak, to the sail boat and the small motor boats, to the "Cruise for a few hours" yacht, all of them waiting patiently for their owners or renters to board for a day at sea.

She then saw the man she and Eli had seen the morning before on the pier, who counted aloud to Eli just how many times he had fished on this vacation; three. In an undertone she said, "You could count this day as number four." She smiled.

True to Dez's expectation, from out of nowhere appeared the typical scene of mother pushing baby in the stroller as they went down the cobblestone side walk. Dez sat there watching them until they were no longer in sight. This scene was a signal for her to either continue writing or to go back to the apartment. She welcomed the interruptions that would impede her from continuing to write about Jake's death. She knew it would stare her in the face and nothing, absolutely nothing would distract her from recalling the events that led up to her finding out about it. *When it was the time to write about it,* she thought, *it would be time.*

Now with all of the distractions depleted, the time had come for her to face the real reason for her being at

Cape Cod. Before writing, she assured herself that there was no letting go, but, rather, a lessening of the tremendous hurt that ensued so wretchedly after the loss of someone as special as a child, be it to death while still in the womb or after reaching the age of twenty-three as in Jake's case, or even losing a child of seventy or even older. The fact that life was snatched out of the order of how a generation comes in and a generation goes out is an added bombardment of hurt feelings experienced by those in such a category: the child dying before the parent.

Death is a tremendous loss to the survivors, no matter which order it comes. Dez had experienced both, and the hurt was dreadful. Somehow, writing about it, letting it out in some form or another would lift the heavy feelings she had carried until present, and thus allow a more tranquil spirit to pervade where it once existed before Jake's death.

As Dez sat alone on the long jetty, arms around her knees with hands clasped together, looking out at the white tipped waves coming ever so softly towards the rocks lining the water's edge as if in slow motion, there, in the distance, she saw the renowned light house with the beautiful back-drop of those perfect infamous scalloped white puffy clouds floating against the blue sky.

Looking at the clouds took Dez back to her high

school days at Hallettsville High. In particular, what she recollected was her Physical Science, Biology, Physics and Chemistry classes. Each year did not pass without the mention of, or a picture of the cirrus, stratus or cumulonimbus clouds.

A collection of the clouds took on a shape of something familiar to Dez, something she had seen in recent weeks while she was preparing for her month's stay on Cape Cod. It was gradually coming back to her, and all of a sudden she saw that the compiled clouds stopped moving and stayed there as if to say, "Not until you remember will we disperse and form yet another resemblance of something."

She continued to watch and allow herself to be perplexed over this view, but when she finally remembered what it was, she laughed to herself. *How could I possibly have seen THAT in these clouds?* She looked back to the clouds to try to make that determination, but the sailboat resemblance had already shifted and moved to form someone else's memories.

She continued to see what else was brought within her view in the distance on the water. It was a cruise ship and the people aboard were waving, trying to get her attention, and continued waving until she finally raised both hands and waved them side to side very slowly so the people aboard would not miss seeing her reciprocate their enthusiastic waving.

Not only did she see the people on board, she

heard a very distinct whistle coming from the cruise ship, not only once, but at least three times, as if they knew they were not heard the previous two times. *Evidently*, she thought to herself, *that person is really excited to be on that cruise ship.* She thought further that the person was enjoying the getaway from life's day-to-day stress with all of its chaotic mayhem and wondered if the cruise actually helped, or was it just more of the same right there on the ship, and they actually had not escaped.

She looked back at the lighthouse and noticed the light blinking on and off to guide cruise ships to dock at just the right designated location. It did not take long after the ship had docked for the stream of passengers to begin their trek to visit the local shops, landmarks for that area, and the restaurants, and of course, to gather souvenirs for their family and friends back home, as if they would be a consolation for not accompanying them on that dream vacation. As she watched the tourists disappear into and reemerge out of the stores in her line of sight she wondered who actually was consoled – the vacationers or those for whom they bought.

She wondered these things because it had not been that long ago that she felt that way, making gift decisions when she and Eli took a 30th Anniversary Foliage Cruise. With so many family members and close friends to consider, she and Eli decided that in order to cover all the bases, they would simply enjoy the cruise and leave the ritual of souvenir hunting to others.

Dez shook her head and could not believe how much thought she had given to those people on the cruise ship and her own cruise experience. At that point, she picked up her notebook and began writing. She kept the notebook with her for those thoughts that would otherwise be lost had she not put them in writing. She called her notebook the 'transfer writing pad'.

If the beautiful display of white puffy clouds against the blue sky, or the lighthouse beckoning the cruise ship, or the cruise ship itself were not enough to distract her from writing any further, the next thing that came along sure did. She turned to keep watchful of her surroundings while alone on the jetty, and there, back on the shore, was a family with twin boys, a beautiful little girl and the parents. Although it distracted her for the remainder of this particular time on the jetty, that scene, that family, inspired her.

She grabbed the writing pad that she had placed on the dull rocks, picked up the pen and then began describing the family that reminded her of her own. The words flowed from her allowing her to continue what she had come to the Cape to do.

Dez had been on Cape Cod for a week and nothing like the present scene had moved her to begin writing about what had happened that lead up to Jake's death, nothing, until this moment.

It had been a week into her month's stay, and now, once again she found herself at the Pier View Restaurant for breakfast after her routine walk. She watched the off-season crowd as she slowly sipped her coffee, and in so doing caught glimpses of the times she and Eli enjoyed, moments like this one, before he left for Texas. She was also able to capture the feelings from their afternoon delights at the Internet Café in Hallettsville. She anticipated continuing to traverse the same path that she and Eli covered while he was in Onset Village.

She could vividly see his smile across the table at the seafood restaurant and the subsequent dimple on his left cheek when she made him laugh about one thing or another.

She then captured the moment when she and Eli held hands crossing the pedestrian crosswalk that was painted green and trimmed on both sides with white paint, then, the cobblestone crosswalk and how he made her feel like a little child being lead to kindergarten. She had tried, at that point, to make him feel the same as if his mother were holding his little toddler hand, leading him to the school bus waiting on the corner. Every now and then her pondering thoughts were interrupted by a bushy tailed squirrel jotting across those crosswalks, appearing not to be afraid of passersby or cars passing ever so slowly, its mind focusing only on getting to its next climb.

What *did* bring her out of her gaze was a couple that walked right past her window, no, not just that couple, but after that, a flood of couples passed, and across the street, she saw a couple locked arm and arm, staring out at the bay and all the boats obediently staying in their locations. The couple looked to be the age of Brant and Suzanna and with that, memories of the two of them together, especially on the night of Arelius' and Adreanna's graduation, made the couple across the street disappear, as her tears flowed when she thought of Brant without her mother.

She left the restaurant, and now as she sat on the jetty, she felt inspired as she intently looked at the family that had come so early to her part of the beach.

They stirred her memory of her own six member family who had gone to the beach and pitched camp the night before, and who, the following morning, were in a contest to see the sunrise first.

The next morning, Dez was at her picture window in the studio apartment, looking out above the grove of trees where she knew to be the location for the sun to make its entrance into Onset Village. It rose into the picture window, having already made its entrance with its orange brightness, only to have changed its appearance to one that only a glimpse was possible because its radiance was too spectacular to look upon.

Also to be seen this particular morning in the near

distance were the historical bed and breakfast Inns with their Victorian style architecture.

Dez continued to write from the previous night, constantly inspired during the night by that inner inspiration that she carried within her mind and now within her heart. It had become a healing power to her once stricken spirit, and now, an inspiration that she would always acknowledge and which had become a real force, so much so that she vowed to keep such inspiration ever ready, to get through whatever came her way. She knew it came not only from the deep confines of her once sought after source from within, but from all the encounters of short arisings in her life.

Eli and Dez would always be reminded of Jake, even though he was no longer with them. It would forever be possible to equate this memory with something that had always been and will always be, for eternity. Some things Jake took delight in with his family were: sunrises, sunsets, and times at the beach. As Brant had brought his past from the crevices of his own mind on many occasions, Dez also would retrieve from the depth of her heart the memory of when she and Eli went to Mustang Island, on a full moon, and with an urn filled with Jake's ashes, let them go in the waves of the Gulf of Mexico, a place Jake loved to go.

This morning, this cool and crisp morning, found Dez once again sitting on the jetty, alone, satisfied with the completion of her writing and waiting for the sunrise as she saw the waves gently coming ashore to greet her. Upon seeing the sun surface above the glistening sea, with the coolness it portrayed with its initial debut, Dez, with tear filled eyes, said, as Jake thirteen years previous had said, "I see it! I see it! I saw the sunrise first!"

At the end of the writing of this trilogy, the author could be found at her country home in Hallettsville, Texas writing her fourth novel...PURE EXISTENCE. This novel has as its main character, Dr. Alex Glendale, as introduced in Volume III of the Encounters of Short Arisings Trilogy, Beyond Encounters. Denice Enoch Craton has endeavored to provide reading enjoyment with a plot of adventure, light mystery, and humor. The main character is writing a novel. The title of the novel within PURE EXISTENCE is entitled, RENDEZVOUS TWELVE.

EXCERPT FROM

PURE EXISTENCE

Once when Alex was called to the hospital, she grabbed notes from her novel that she was eventually going to incorporate into her story. Because her mind was on getting to the mother in labor, as she passed the doctor's lounge, she sat her folder on the table and hastily went to the delivery room without a thought of anyone looking at them, after all, it was after hours and things were quiet on her floor.

It was an open opportunity for anyone who had been interested in her writings to get a peek at her new hobby of writing. Several of her colleagues within the hospital and a few friends outside the hospital knew of her new venture, and when they would ask her about it, her constant reply was, "when I'm done, I'll share."

By far the majority was willing to wait, however one colleague was eager to know about her writings. It was information that would in some way help in his endeavor to persuade her to leave her house, to vacate it permanently.

Although Dr. Cooperston's office was on the fourteenth floor, he would make it his business to visit the lounge on the twelfth floor where Dr. Glendale's office was located. His reason was for the coffee. To the doctors in the lounge on the twelfth floor he would often say, "Whoever made this coffee should come and do the same for us in the lounge on the fourteenth floor."

No one ever thought he had an ulterior motive in visiting their lounge; in fact a few of the doctors from the twelfth floor lounge agreed with him about the coffee from his lounge and thought nothing of his presence on their floor.

It would be good timing on Dr. Cooperston's part to have frequented the twelfth floor lounge this particular time when Dr. Glendale had brought notes from her novel and left them in the main lounge, the one she never goes to because she has her own.

To his amazement, there sitting on the table was Alex's notes. It was after hours but the coffee was fresh and its aroma made for pleasing expressions to any whose noses met its whiff. One such nose was Dr. Cooperston's.

He had the added pleasure of glancing through Alex's notes from her novel, Rendezvous Twelve.

"It's what I've needed to push her over the edge and get her out of the house that should have been mine. I have to be careful. Yes, I'll make copies and read them at home. I'll keep them in my attic with my other important things."

Just as he was copying the notes, Barry Gardinsky came into the lounge.

"Hello Dr. Cooperston," said Mr. Gardinsky.

Dr. Cooperston was shocked to hear his name called and so turned abruptly and after seeing Mr. Gardinsky said, "Mr. Gardinsky, what a surprise to see you."

"I must say, I too am surprised to see you here on the twelfth floor. Are you on standby to deliver babies?" asked Mr. Gardinsky in a kidding manner.

All the while Dr. Cooperston was talking with Mr. Gardinsky he was fidgeting with Alex's notes, stacking them and then returning them to her folder. He set it back on the table and turned the folder face down.

Mr. Gardinsky could not help noticing the front of the folder because of a familiar name on it along with what appeared to be a title, it read, Rendezvous Twelve a Novel by Alex Glendale.

It was the doctor's demeanor that gave Mr. Gardinsky the feeling that he was up to something. He just looked out of place, thought Mr. Gardinsky.

He didn't make any reference to the folder and made sure he focused face to face with Dr. Cooperston as he felt he had come in on something. Mr. Gardinsky had feelings similar to those he had the day he met Dr. Cooperston. Dr. Glendale recommended Dr. Cooperston to him the day he mistook her to be a male doctor. He seemed distracted during his entire visit and remembered he didn't even ask him to do the usual cough he had practiced while waiting for Dr. Alex Glendale in one of her patient rooms.

Once again, Mr. Gardinsky thought that something was suspicious about this doctor. What exactly he did not know. But he was beginning to think it involved Dr. Glendale because she had become a topic of their conversation during his exam. Mr. Gardinsky remembered thinking during one point of the visit, "He seems to be more interested in what I know about Dr. Glendale than me as a patient."

To confirm his feelings about the hasty first doctor visit, Dr. Cooperston asked, "Mr. Gardinsky, how are you today? I must apologize about the quick physical I conducted on you the other day. There were a few other things I should have checked and I would like you to come back. Only if there are additional tests will I charge you. The visit will cost you nothing. Would you agree to the follow up visit?"

Had Mr. Gardinsky not met the doctor at this time, he had no intentions of seeing him again due to the fact that he felt short changed with his physical. His intentions were to inform Dr. Glendale of his decision since she referred him to Dr. Cooperston.

Before he could answer, Dr. Glendale appeared

in the doorway and before speaking to either of the men, made a dash for her folder. It didn't go without her notice that it wasn't in the exact spot she had left it. Some strange feeling came over her that at least one of them had opened it. She shrugged the idea so as not to appear overly concerned about who did or did not look at her novel.

"Dr. Cooperston, Mr. Gardinsky," she greeted the both of them.

"Dr. Glendale," said Mr. Gardinsky.

"Dr. Glendale, are you just arriving?" asked Dr. Cooperston.

With that question, Dr. Glendale is assuming Mr. Gardinsky had been there before Dr. Cooperston, and therefore was responsible for relocating her folder.

"No, I've been here long enough to deliver a little girl. What brings you two to the twelfth floor?"

"I just got here and was about to get coffee. Your doctor's lounge has the reputation for having the best coffee," said Dr. Cooperston.

"And Mr. Gardinsky, what brings you here?"

"First, may I give an answer to Dr. Cooperston, I

was about to before you came in."

"Sure, excuse my interrupting."

"It's a welcomed one I assure you."

Turning to Dr. Cooperston, Mr. Gardinsky said "Yes, I appreciate that. I would like that very much."

"Good," said Dr. Cooperston, just call the office; they will expect your call. Well, I'd better get going; it's been a long day."

"You're coffee?" asked Mr. Gardinsky.

"Right, thank you," said the doctor.

Even though it turned for the better, Mr. Gardinsky was still going to tell Alex about his first visit, and most definitely he was going to set things straight about what the doctor said about his just getting there.

Dr. Cooperston got his coffee and left.

"I appreciate your patience, Dr. Glendale," said Barry.

"It's ok. What brings you here?"

"I'm sure you must know, the only connection I have to the twelfth floor is you," said Barry.

"I would have thought that, yes."

"So what brought me here is you. I wanted to talk

with you about something that's been on my mind ever since you sent me to the fourteenth floor to see Dr. Cooperston. And when I came here and saw him in this lounge I was very surprised."

"He was here before you?" asked Alex.

"Yes, he was, and he was at the copier making copies of what you have there clutched in your arms."

"He was? Why would be copying my novel?"

"That's a very good question. My question to you is, why would you be a topic of his and my conversation that day in his office when I went for my physical?" asked Barry.

"Is there something going on between the two of you that perhaps I should know about. I'm wondering if I should ask you to join some friends and me on a cruise.

"No way," exclaimed Alex.

"No way about you and him, or no way about joining my friends and me?" asked Barry.

"I thought you were here first the way he put it."

"I think it's what he wanted you to believe."

"Personally, and to be frank, I think I caught him red handed making copies of papers from your folder."

"That's strange. And in answer to your question, no way about him and me."

"That's a welcomed relief," sighed Barry with a heavy breath.

"Oh?" asked Alex.

"Well, had it been, I'd be saying goodbye about now," said Barry.

"Had it been, we wouldn't have had dinner," replied Alex.

"Tu shay," said Barry.

"I'm not sure I want to approach Dr. Cooperston about looking at my notes."

"If it were that he was merely looking at them, maybe not. But I stood in the doorway long enough to know he was copying them. He folded what he had and put them in the inside pocket of his coat. The originals he hastily put in the folder and placed it face down on the table, no doubt in a place you didn't leave it."

"You're right about the big difference in looking at them verses copying them. I just have no idea why he would do that."

"You'll wonder until you ask him. Would you like

me to accompany you?"